THE WHITE KNIGHT

K.B. KIRTLEY

First Edition

Cover Design by MIBL Art
(or however MIBL Art prefers its credits)

ISBN 979-8-9898780-0-0 (paperback)

ISBN 979-8-9898780-1-7 (ebook)

Published by Kirtley Books

www.kirtleybooks.com

Dedication

For my dad – My first hero. My very own Superman. The man who introduced me to this beautiful world of heroes and villains and the stories they tell and has been asking me when this book would be published so he could have a copy for almost a decade. It's finally here.

ONE

"Somebody help!"

The scream shattered the silence of the still night. Lance leapt from the table he was sitting at, leaving his chair rocking in his wake as he rushed to the fire escape. He dropped to the ground, hitting only every third rung on the ladder in his hurry. He let go of the fire escape with five rungs to go and landed with a thud on the cold grass. The courtyard sitting underneath the balcony was dark on that cloudy night, a result of the campus having few lights outside most of its buildings. He sprinted toward the source of the scream, pulling the nightstick from his hoodie pocket as he ran across the courtyard.

He had almost made it the full length of the grassy courtyard to where the two figures were intertwined when a man jumped backward and cursed, tucking his right hand under the opposite arm and leaving behind a woman still lying on the ground. Lance could hear him mumbling something about having been bit as he closed in on the man. His concern over his hand quickly disappeared, though, as he backed into Lance, swinging the nightstick into the back of his knees.

A scream laced with pain and fear escaped the man's lips as he crumpled to the ground at Lance's feet.

"Wh-Wh-Who are you?" the man asked, looking up from his curled fetal position, clutching the back of each leg.

The man was no more than five-foot-eight, at least half a foot shorter than Lance's six-foot-two and appeared to be in much worse shape. Lance had kept an athletic build since his playing days had abruptly ended and was still more fit than many of the small college's athletes.

Lance ignored the man's question, instead asking a question of his own in barely more than a whisper, "Is this the first time you've attacked someone on this campus?"

Lance circled the man and pulled the hood of his hoodie up to better hide his face. The man quickly looked away without responding. Lance waited a moment for him to speak before striking the man's injured hand with the nightstick.

"Ahh!" the man howled in pain as he rolled away from Lance, grasping at his hand again.

"Answer me," Lance growled, raising his intensity but not his voice. "Is this the first time you've attacked someone?"

"No," he panted, "I did it once before. Just once, I swear! it wasn't even an attack. We were at a house party, and we were both pretty drunk, but I was still functioning. She wasn't. She was into me, and I was into her, but that wasn't good enough for the misconduct office, so I got a strike for assault. I don't go around trying to hurt people!"

"Then, how do you explain what happened here tonight?" Lance asked, still speaking softly enough on the windy night that only the man could hear what he was saying.

"I saw her studying in the union. When she got up to leave, I tried to shoot my shot and talk to her. She blew me off and left. I followed her outside and reached for her shoulder to try and explain. It's late, and it can be dangerous out here at night. But as soon as I touched her shoulder, she screamed. I panicked and tried to cover her mouth. I know I shouldn't have done that, but I got scared. Then you showed up, trying to be a hero. I was just trying to talk to her. Hey, are you even listening to me?" the man asked sharply as Lance paced back and forth beside him without looking down.

Lance made it clear that he had been listening, though, when, just seconds after the man finished talking, Lance used his nightstick again, this time causing the man to slump unconsciously to the ground as Lance struck him in the head. Lance turned away from him and walked back to the young woman who had stood from where she had fallen and had been watching their exchange from a distance.

He stopped short of where she stood. He stared straight ahead, standing perpendicular to her and making sure his hood was pulled down enough that she couldn't see his face.

"Are you hurt?" he grumbled in a tone much lower than his natural voice as he looked at her out of the corner of his eye, waiting for her answer.

The first thing he noticed as he glanced over was how short she was, maybe a little over five feet tall. Her black hair framed her pale face, letting the dim light illuminate her features. He looked away again and stumbled on.

"I mean, I know you must be pretty shaken up, but did he physically hurt you or anything? Do I need to call an ambulance or anything?"

"Not that I can tell," she responded, rubbing her neck and holding her backpack close to her chest. "I know that as far as pain goes, he got it worse than I did. I bit his hand right before you arrived." She finished with a small smile.

"I'm sure that must have tasted awful," Lance answered with a brief smile in her direction before shaking his head at the comment. "Can you call the police while I make sure he can't leave if he wakes up?" He turned to walk toward the man, who was still unconscious where Lance had left him.

"Sure!" she called out after him as he walked away.

She pulled her cell phone out of her backpack and turned away from the two men. Lance lifted the man off the ground and pulled a ball of rope from his hoodie, securing the attacker's hands and feet and setting him in a chair at one of the courtyard's tables.

"So, does my hero have a name?" she asked with a grin as she put her phone away and turned back around to find only her unconscious attacker tied up in a chair.

Lance walked back through the courtyard again early the next morning to get breakfast with Gwen and Hailey at the student union. The courtyard looked drastically different in the daylight. The bright green grass and trees beginning to blossom were surrounded by students on blankets sprawled across the grass, in hammocks, and sitting on the benches and tables scattered around the square. Dark red brick buildings sat on every side of the courtyard—the library on the west end, the language arts building on the south end, and the L-shaped student union on the north and east borders.

As he made his way through the packed tables to the food court, he quickly learned that his vigilantism the night before had received more publicity than he had expected. He imagined that the only people who would find out about what had happened would be some of the victim's closest friends. As he neared the food court, though, he found that the entire student body was discussing what had happened in the courtyard last night. He picked up a copy of the Franklin Gazette, the school's student newspaper, and looked for the article. It took him only long enough to unfold the paper. The story was at the bottom of the front page, next to a photo of the chair and rope used to tie the man up.

As Lance waited in line to get his breakfast at the union's little café, he read the article.

NEW HERO ON CAMPUS

It appears that our campus might have found itself a new guardian, if last night's incident was any indication. At 1:30 am last night, Jessica Li, a freshman on the gymnastics team, began making her way back to her residence hall after a night of preparing for a test in the student union. "I got a weird feeling as I left the union," she admitted, standing in the courtyard where she was attacked. "I felt like I was being followed, so I started walking faster." Jessica was not walking for long, though, as her attacker, who will be left unnamed as requested by campus police as they further investigate the incident, struck. "One moment, I was walking across the union courtyard, feeling slightly uneasy, after a guy I had never met tried talking to me as I was leaving a study group late last night. It was nothing too out of the ordinary, but after I had gotten outside, someone grabbed me by the shoulder and was trying to cover my mouth with the opposite hand. He began pulling me down before he covered my mouth, and I screamed as I left my feet." It was that scream that seemingly alerted our hero.

Lance took his eyes off the page long enough to order a coffee and banana muffin. He knew he had recognized that backpack. Franklin's student-athletes were all given the same backpack. The gymnastics team was one of the top-ranked schools in the nation, and they were led by a freshman with a shot at the Olympics. *That explains why everyone is so interested in what happened,* Lance thought to himself before reading on.

I was able to get him off of me a little after I bit his hand, and I guess that was enough as someone came and took out his legs.' After taking out the attacker's legs, Jessica said the vigilante talked to the attacker for a moment, though she could not hear any of their conversation through last night's strong winds, before knocking him out and returning his attention to her. Jessica said that, after checking on her, he requested that she call the police. By the time she had finished her call, her hero had vanished, leaving her unconscious attacker tied to a chair. The police arrived soon after and took the man into custody. 'I only wish I had the time to thank him last night.' Jessica lamented to me as I wrapped up the interview. So, to whoever our new unnamed campus hero is, on behalf of Jessica, myself, and the rest of the student body, thank you.

Hailey Hall

He looked up from the article as he crossed the room and saw them sitting on the same side of a booth along the union's south wall. He headed for the table with his breakfast, tucking the paper underneath his arm as he walked.

Hailey was the taller of the two. At just over five-ten, she was even taller than a lot of the guys around campus. She had dark brown hair and amber eyes that complemented her Cherokee features and tan skin. Her hair was cut shorter than Lance's shaggy black hair. She had been a nationally ranked distance runner in high school and continued to run regularly even now that she was no longer competing.

Next to her, Gwen stood in sharp contrast. Gwen was shorter, only five-foot-three, and was almost pale in her complexion with light-brown hair that ran past her shoulders and green eyes that shone bright like emeralds against her skin. Gwen had never been much of an athlete or really into sports at all, for that matter. She would go to Lance's games in high school, but only to support her friend.

"Great article, Hall. Gripping. Suspenseful. Maybe work on getting a more fully fleshed-out lead character next time. Otherwise, it was a smashing article," Lance teased as he tossed the paper on the table and sat across from the girls with a smile to Gwen, who responded only with an exaggerated eye roll.

"Thanks, Locke!" Hailey responded, smiling as she rolled her eyes. "I know that you're being sarcastic, but this actually was one of my favorite stories I've gotten to write, so I'm just going to pretend you were actually being sincere for once. This is the kind of story I've been wanting to cover. I always have to write about how some violent crime happened on campus, so writing about how a violent crime was stopped by some do-gooder is a really nice change of pace."

Lance shrugged off Hailey's jab with a smile. "Jessica seemed pretty talkative for someone who had been attacked not too long beforehand. What did you have to bribe her with to get her to talk?"

"Lance, I know you don't respect me as a journalist, but do you really think that I would stoop so low as to bribe someone just, so I could get a good story?"

"Hailey, Hailey, Hailey," Lance started. "It's not that I don't respect you—I just don't respect your profession as a whole. Everything has to be sensational, and it's usually sensationally negative. It has nothing to do with how I see you. I actually think you're one of the best. Or one of the worst. I never can really figure out how those in your profession view those who try to tell the truth. Either way, you're on that side, and I truly have the utmost respect for you."

"Getting her to talk really wasn't that difficult once she found out that she would get to be in the paper today.

I hadn't covered the gymnastics team, but from what I remember, she was always willing to give a quote. Plus, she seemed quite fond of her mystery man."

"I know you got more than what was in the article. What else did she tell you about our hidden hero? Our secret savior? Our guarded guardian, if you will."

Hailey waited for Gwen to stop laughing. "Are you finished?"

"What?" Gwen asked. "It was funny . . ."

Lance wasn't sure if it was Hailey's disapproving glare or his smug smirk that had more to do with Gwen trailing off.

"Back to our knight in shining armor, Jessica wasn't able to tell me much. That courtyard is notoriously dark, and with the clouds last night, it was even darker, so she couldn't even give us a rough idea of what he looked like. Just that he had some sort of stick he was carrying around, that he saved her, and that he vanished without her noticing. You know, textbook heroism."

"I wish I could be a hero. I would most definitely stick around to take the credit," Lance announced before taking a bite from his muffin.

"I'm sure you would, Lance," Hailey said with an eye roll, "You couldn't even give a five-minute presentation last semester in Spanish."

"Hey! That's not fair. I wouldn't be speaking Spanish. I would be speaking English. And English is a language that I know, like, at least a triple-digit number of words that I can use."

"Help me out here, Gwen," Hailey pleaded. "Tell Lance that, even if he was a hero, he certainly wouldn't stay and talk to the press."

Gwen looked up from the toast she had been spreading her grape jelly on while the other two went back and forth, "I don't know, Lance might give you an exclusive interview."

Lance laughed while reaching his hand across the table to give Gwen a high-five. "That's right, Hailey!" he gloated. "Dream team for the last twenty-one years. Can't split us up!"

"But, no." Gwen laughed. "There's no chance you would stay for any kind of press. You probably wouldn't have talked to the attacker or the victim either unless you had already known them for years."

"HA!" Hailey shouted. "Take that, Locke!"

After taking his time with an extra big bite of his muffin, Lance shifted the topic back onto the vigilante. "So, you told me how Jessica felt about the vigilante, but what about you? How do you feel about this new guardian, Hall? Do you really think it's someone trying to be a hero or just someone being at the right place at the right time?"

"I think it's a little of both. Obviously, this guy would have to have been at the right place at the right time, but I think most people wouldn't have rushed to Jessica's side even if they were there at the right time. Plus, what are the odds someone just happened to be taking a stroll with a weapon like that and just happened to be out there at one-thirty at night? I'm going to say the odds aren't that high. So, yeah, I think our campus does have itself a hero, Locke. Gwen, what do you think about this vigilante? Hero? Or nothing but a shy Good Samaritan?"

"I—" Her words caught in her mouth. She paused as Lance watched her, his smiling fading. "I want to believe that there is someone who is tired of seeing the pain on this campus and has decided to do something about it. That there is someone who is trying to watch over the campus now. That seems to be the more hopeful of the two options, so I think I'm going to side with Hailey on this one as well."

Lance stood from the table as Gwen finished. "I can't believe what you've done, Hailey Hall," he declared, balling up his muffin holder and putting it in his empty coffee cup. "You have turned my best friend against me, and for that, I can never forgive you."

"Oh well. We were never really that close anyway." Hailey shrugged as she took a sip of coffee.

"Are we still on to go get our gowns for graduation tomorrow? Even with your pain of being betrayed so fresh?" Gwen asked with a smile, her gloom only momentary.

"I guess," Lance sighed. "I'll see you then!"

Lance made his way to the gym after his quick breakfast. He had never expected his attempt at protecting the campus to lead to anything. Not really. After having to actually fight someone, he realized that he wasn't nearly as prepared as he had originally thought. Protecting his campus would require him to be fit enough to defend others in a way he couldn't right now. He got lucky in his first fight. He caught the attacker by surprise and that he wasn't in the best shape in his own right. *Still*, Lance thought to himself, *I can't expect to protect others in the shape that I am in right now.*

He started his workout with some stretching before doing anything else. Lance had spent little time in the gym since the injury that had derailed his once-promising baseball career his senior year of high school. He had stayed in decent shape by playing intramurals and his new habit of patrolling the campus by night, but he was also beginning to see the effects of not spending time in the gym in the softness of his arms and stomach.

Lance started with a run after his stretches. Since he had stayed in relatively good shape, he was able to run a mile and a half before he began to wear down. Next, he made his way over to the weightlifting area of the gym and found the pull-up bar. After following that up with chin-ups, squats, and the rowing machine, Lance was exhausted. He made his way up the stairs and to the little smoothie bar next to the door to get a protein shake on his way home. After making it back to his unmade bed, Lance collapsed and took a three-hour nap before his one class of the day.

Lance headed straight to the cafeteria after getting out of his class to meet up with his roommates for dinner. As he waited in line to pay, he overheard the group in front of him and the one behind him talking about the events from the previous night.

"I know what you mean." Lance heard one of the students behind him agreeing. "I feel less safe knowing that there is some loon running around trying to deliver his own twisted form of justice. There is a reason we have cops on campus. He needs to let them do their jobs."

"The cops wouldn't have been any help last night," another group member reminded. "All they could have done was try to find the attacker to punish him after something had happened. And most of the time, they're not even able to do that much. The vigilante was able to stop anything from happening to the girl, catch the guy, and get him locked up. I don't know what more you could want from him."

Lance nodded in agreement as this girl talked.

"I want less from him, not more. I think this guy's probably in over his head, and he's going to end up getting someone hurt."

The little that Lance could hear from the group in front of him was much more encouraging. While he couldn't hear their full conversation, he did hear the words "thankful," "protected," and "hero" all more than once.

Finally able to pay, Lance grabbed a burger and fries and looked for Taylor and Jason in the crowded tables.

"What's up, guys?" Lance asked as he sat after finding them tucked back into a corner. "I got breakfast with Hailey and Gwen this morning, Jason. Hailey was pretty excited about her article today. I'm assuming she gave you the unedited version?"

"Yeah." Jason sighed. "And trust me, they did a lot of editing to get it down to the size of that article. She talked about it for an hour at lunch and only stopped because she got a call from her editor wanting her to go in after she ate. Something about having some project he thought she would like."

"What do you think about this vigilante?" Taylor asked Lance.

Jason and Taylor made Gwen and Hailey look like sisters by comparison. Jason was six-foot-four and two hundred twenty-five pounds of muscle. He had black hair he cut himself twice a week that stayed close to his head, dark brown eyes, and chestnut skin. Taylor, at five-nine and a hundred forty pounds, was the smallest of their group, other than Gwen. He had shaggy dirty-blonde hair and the same green eyes and pale skin as his cousin.

"I'm not sure where I stand on him yet," Lance answered. "I guess my biggest hold up with this whole thing is whether he's actually trying to be a hero or if he just happened to be in the area at the time. I mean, if he is trying to be a hero, great, this campus desperately needs one. But I think it's too early to jump to that definitive conclusion."

"I think he is trying to be a hero, and I think it's great that someone is finally worried enough about this campus's safety to do something about it. This is what? The twenty-third straight year we've been in the top ten most violent universities? Someone finally decided that enough is enough and is taking the matter into their own hands. More power to him. I have half a mind to throw on one of my old hoodies and join him out there."

"I'm not so sure, Jason," Taylor began, "We know nothing about this guy and—"

"Of course we know nothing about him!" Jason said. "Otherwise, he wouldn't be able to do any of this! If people knew who he was, there would be all sorts of pressure and criticism on him. You wouldn't be able to get on the internet without seeing a dozen hot takes on him. Not to mention the administration would quickly put an end to his whole crusade. It only works if we know nothing about him."

"That may be so, but the fact remains that this guy could end up adding to our violence and crime just as much as he takes away from it, if not more. That is, if he really is trying to take away from the violence in the first place. I just think we're putting too much faith in this one act," Taylor cautioned.

"Well," Jason added, "good or bad, I'm sure we'll begin to know more soon enough."

And with that, the conversation switched to their usual topics of classes, sports, and their outlooks with only three months until graduation.

As they finished eating and walked to return their plates, Jason turned to Lance. "Me and Taylor are about to head to the gym if you want to join. We're going to play some racquetball."

"I appreciate the offer, but I went earlier for a workout, and I'm feeling pretty sore. First time I've done an actual routine in a while, and I'm feeling the effects. Maybe next time!"

"Looks like Jason is just going to have to lose by himself again then," Taylor said as they walked out into the setting sun.

"I'm winning this time. No way I'm letting you beat me for the fourth straight time."

"This will actually be the fifth straight time."

"Whatever the streak is, it ends today. We'll catch you later, Lance!" Jason called as they walked away with a wave.

Lance returned the wave and headed back to the apartment. He was actually feeling pretty good after his workout earlier, but he had to prepare to go out again tonight. If this campus thought they needed a hero, then a hero was what he would give them.

chapter

TWO

Lance rubbed at his eyes after an hour-long nap. The clock read midnight as he rolled out of bed, dropping to a knee on the cold wood floor. Reaching under the bed, he pulled out the old wooden box his dad had given him for his birthday seven years earlier. He tossed the box on the bed and slowly got dressed in the dark room. Still wearing the jeans from the day before, he grabbed a black long-sleeved shirt from his closet and laced up his shoes. Returning to his bed, he unlatched the lid of the old oak box and opened it to pull out his father's old nightstick. Dressed and with the nightstick in hand, Lance grabbed his hoodie from off the back of his desk chair and silently left the apartment.

When he began his late-night rounds on campus, he was always afraid he would wake Jason or Taylor when he was leaving the apartment. After a couple of months now without them catching on, though, he was no longer worried about being too loud. They were both sound asleep by this time every night. They both had an eight AM class every weekday, and staying up into the early morning hours playing games had come to an end with their junior year when they realized they would join the real world soon. Lance should have been most worried about getting rest for school. Jason and Taylor both carried strong GPAs and had their next steps already lined up, but here he was, leaving the room in the middle of the night to go play hero.

As Lance started walking away from his apartment, he noticed that he was once again making his way toward the library. He didn't have a planned path or any real structure for these nightly patrols; he just kind of wandered around campus for the most part. It seemed fitting, though, that the stretch to and from the library was how he started and ended each night. It was Gwen's walk on this short stretch early last December that had started his crusade.

Lance made a circle around the library and then continued on to the union balcony, his preferred spot to camp when he was out at night. The balcony had no lights, so there were no students there studying at night, and it was difficult to see up onto it when it was dark out due to the backdrop of the union. Wearing his dark jeans and black hoodie, Lance was undetectable. It also afforded him a great place to watch over campus as it allowed him to see the entrance to the library in the distance, the entrance to the union to the right, and the courtyard underneath. He saw students standing on the balcony as he drew near tonight, though. His heroics the night before had created more than just gossip. People wanted to find this vigilante and prove—or disprove—his existence.

Lance slowly backed up and made his way back toward the library. There wasn't a single positive that Lance could think of coming from people knowing he was the campus hero, but there were plenty of negatives. The unwanted attention would make doing this more difficult, probably impossible. The administration wouldn't let him continue his patrols in a best-case scenario, and expulsion would be more likely. Everything he had ever done or said would be dug up and pored over to either prop him up into an infallible do-gooder or a villain that was worse than any threat he could take down. And, though he wouldn't admit this to them, Gwen and Hailey were right: he would hate the attention that would come with being known as the vigilante.

Beyond what everyone else on campus would think if they found out he was the vigilante, what would his closest friends think? Jason would be mad at Lance for not inviting him on his adventure. He wanted to join the vigilante without knowing who it was. If he knew it was his best friend, and he wasn't included, there would be hurt feelings, at the very least. Taylor wouldn't be much happier, but he would be more upset with Lance for breaking rules and taking justice into his own hands than with not being invited along. He could hear Taylor now, asking him what his father, a career cop, would think about him shirking the law like this.

Lance spat at the thought of that conversation. Hailey would be disappointed that she hadn't gotten that exclusive with him before it went public. Lance was sure Hailey would think that breaking a story like this could be her big break. And what about Gwen? She would feel guilty, responsible even. She probably—*no.* Lance shook his head. He would not run through what Gwen would think or what she would feel about finding out it was him. He would not torment himself in that way. Not anymore. *It's not important anyway*, he assured himself. *No one needs to know who is under the hood.* He had done a good job concealing his identity last night, and if anything else happens, that will be priority number two after helping whoever needs help.

He found a small picnic table tucked into the shadows outside of the library where he could see out, but it would be difficult for others to see him. He set the nightstick on the table as he lowered himself into the seat and looked for signs that anything was out of the ordinary. There weren't too many students coming to the library this late at night, not with midterms having passed, so it was quiet.

When his phone buzzed in his pocket to let him know that it was now fifteen minutes to three, he got up from the table and stretched. Rubbing at his eyes after staring out into nothing for two hours, he began his short journey back to his apartment. He kept to the shadows to avoid being seen on his way back, but it wasn't necessary—he didn't see a single student on his return trip. He crept back into his room to get more sleep before his ten-thirty class later that morning.

He left his class at eleven-twenty and made his way to the student union. With an hour to kill before the rest of his classes that day, he and Gwen were meeting up for lunch. His class wasn't far from the union, so he arrived fifteen minutes early. He bought himself a chicken sandwich from one of the small food court restaurants and found a booth along the outer wall. He had finished the first half of his sandwich when Gwen walked up.

"Hey!" Gwen greeted with a smile, dropping her bag onto the seat. "How has your day been so far? I see you started without me."

"Hey!" Lance returned. "It's been pretty good. I've only had one class so far, though, so I haven't really gotten started yet. And, yeah, sorry. I was starving. I didn't eat breakfast."

"That's fine." She chuckled. "I understand. What are you doing tomorrow night? One of Hailey's friends is having a party, and we were wondering if you guys wanted to go with us! Jason already said he would, but I doubt Taylor will want to join if you don't go."

"I'm not sure," Lance answered hesitantly. "I have quite a bit of studying for my test next week. And you know I haven't ever really been much into going to parties or anything like that."

"Okay." She sighed. "I understand. It's just that I always feel a little out of place tagging along with Hailey and Jason. You know how they can get. Between the two of them, they know pretty much everyone on campus, and they start working the room the moment they walk through the door. I rarely know more than a couple of other people at the party, and it's hard to keep up with the power couple all night. But it's okay. I understand if you need to work on your school stuff. I'm sure that it will all be fine. I am probably being too dramatic about it all."

Lance ran his fingers through his hair and looked at her as she looked down at the table. He may not have enjoyed parties, but they weren't half as bad as feeling as he was letting Gwen down. He took a deep breath and responded before he could change his mind. "I guess I could go for a little while. But I can't stay too late. I really do have stuff I need to work on."

"Really?" Gwen exclaimed. "That's great! I can't wait!" She finished with a smile lighting up her face.

"Me either," Lance responded, albeit with much less enthusiasm, though a small smile did force itself onto his face as he saw how happy he had made Gwen.

Gwen went to get her lunch and Lance bit into his sandwich again. If *there is a party tomorrow night, then Jason definitely won't be in until late, and if Taylor goes, then he could be out later than usual, too.* He knew that, sooner or later, they would get in late and mess up his routine, but he still hadn't figured out how to work around that to keep them from noticing he was out. He was lost in his own thoughts and hadn't realized Gwen had sat back down and was giving him a concerned look.

"Are you okay, Lance?" she asked, placing her hand on the table, her fingers less than an inch from his. "You've seemed a little bit off the last couple of months since coming back from the break. You have bags under your eyes, and you seem distant a lot, like you're not all the way here. Is everything okay? I don't mean to push. I'm just a little worried about you, and I know the others have noticed it, too."

"Thanks for sugarcoating my appearance. I have a very fragile ego, you know."

"You know I didn't mean it like that. I just meant—"

"I'm kidding, Gwen. Really, I'm fine. I swear," Lance assured her with a smile.

"Okay." Gwen looked away to eat some of her sandwich.

Lance picked his own sandwich back up as the two sat in silence. He could tell that Gwen didn't fully buy he was fine. But he took solace in knowing that Gwen hated conflict enough that the topic probably wouldn't be brought up again anytime soon. Still, he didn't want her worrying herself over him, so he needed to come up with some answer.

"That wasn't completely true," he said as he sat his sandwich down and gave Gwen his full attention. "I'm not a hundred-percent fine. I am starting to get a little nervous about where I'll be in four months. Taylor has already gotten into med school and Jason has been offered an incredible starting job at Fox Corp. I mean, I assume I'll follow them to Duncan, but I really have no idea what I'll do once I get there."

"You still have months to figure out what you want to do. You're acting like you did senior year of high school all over again. You're worrying for no reason and making yourself sick."

"There was plenty of reason to worry then and there is plenty of reason to worry now, too. The only difference is that then I had my scholarship offers all drying up instead of not having any options to begin with."

"At least you're not having to walk around with your shoulder in a brace this time," Gwen pointed out. "Plus, it worked out last time. If you had gone to Duncan to play baseball instead of Franklin, your life would be completely different now. You and Taylor wouldn't have become such good friends. You probably would have never met Jason and Hailey. And we wouldn't have gotten to hang out nearly as often. I think it worked out for the best."

"I guess you're right." He shrugged. "I haven't heard of any vigilantes up at Duncan either, so I guess we have that on them. Speaking of the vigilante, what do you think about him now that you've had another day to think about it?" Lance asked.

He may not want the whole campus's attention on him, and he may not even want her to know that it is him underneath that hood, but he would be lying to say that he wasn't enjoying Gwen's praise, even if she didn't realize it was him that she was giving it to.

"I still feel like he's a hero. I've heard that a lot of people think he just happened to be there, but I don't think so. I think he was out there making sure that something like what was about to happen wouldn't happen. I mean, I guess we won't know unless it keeps happening, but I do think there is someone watching over the campus now. I feel safer now, at least a little bit. I know that's silly, but I feel like this is something good for our campus. That's not something we get a lot here. That's special. I don't know; maybe you could say I'm too optimistic or naive, but I prefer being hopeful to fearful, and if that makes me naive, so be it. So, yes, I do believe someone is watching over us."

Lance nodded as she talked, trying to keep an even demeanor. *She thinks I'm a hero!* Even if she didn't know it was him she was talking about, knowing she felt even remotely safe again on campus for probably the first time in at least the last three months made his late nights worth it.

"I agree," Lance said. "I think that it's impossible to know right now if this guy is for real or if it's just a one-night thing, but it definitely feels real. And, for the time being at least, campus does feel safer."

Gwen smiled as she nodded in agreement, glad that Lance seemed to understand what she had been trying to say. Lance checked his watch and then jumped out of his chair.

"I have to go!" he exclaimed, scrambling for his bag. "I've got class in seven! I will see you in class later. Save me a seat?"

"I can do that! I'll see you then!" she called out as he hurried away.

Lance made his now familiar walk from his apartment to the library again that night like he had every other night since coming back to campus after winter break. Still on a high from hearing Gwen talk about how much the hero means to her, he tried to examine why it was still worth trying to be the campus vigilante, even with all the new attention and pressure.

Gwen. That was, unsurprisingly, the first thing that came to his mind. She was why he became the vigilante. He tried to think of other reasons it was worth continuing to do this beyond the easy answer. As much as he hated to admit it, his guilt from that night had as much to do with him wearing the hood as protecting Gwen did. He wasn't there to protect her when she needed him, and he didn't want anyone else put in the position she was. There was also a sense of vengeance that drove him. As if somehow he would get justice for what had happened by taking out others who would attack the students on campus. The praise wasn't bad either, he thought. Even if no one knew who was saving people, they were all thankful someone was out there. Actually, he preferred the anonymity of his fame.

Lance passed by the union to see a collection of students on the courtyard balcony for the second night in a row. He slipped into the union and found a small study room on the second floor that was unoccupied. He left his backpack with his textbook on the table before sneaking back out of the union. He made a trip around the campus perimeter, starting at the union and going counterclockwise.

While walking along one of the roads creating the campus's boundary, he heard a commotion from the other side of the street that caught his attention. Shouts and what sounded like a trash can being thrown down were enough to spur him to respond. The noise sounded like it had come from behind Ollie's Bar and Lance rushed across the street to see what was happening.

When he got to the back side of the bar, he found four men in the alley, three of them standing over the fourth. Lance pulled his nightstick out of his hoodie as he crept up from behind the group. The three standing were laughing at and taunting the one on the ground.

"Definitely the toughest house."

He heard one of them laugh and slur his words as he kicked the boy. Lance had seen enough. None of the three were small, but they all appeared to be drunk, and Lance had enough training growing up that, even sober, none would stand too much of a chance against him.

He caught the one closest to him with two quick swings of his nightstick: one going up through his knees, causing him to fall backward, and the second coming down into his chest as he fell. As the second man immediately rushed him, Lance lifted his leg and kicked the man in the chest, sending him careening into the wall before he fell to the ground as well. The third man took a slower approach, not wanting to make the same mistake he had seen his friend make. Lance could smell the liquor even from this distance, and when he finally rushed in and threw a right hook at Lance, Lance took a step back and hit the man across the back with his nightstick. The man on the ground against the wall groaned and Lance looked back as a door opened from the bar and took off across the street, quickly disappearing into the campus's shadows that he was just as comfortable navigating in the dark as he was during the daylight.

Lance got back to the study room in the union at one o'clock and texted Hailey to ask what was going on. He told her he had heard a lot of talk in the union about another vigilante sighting. *Come to Ollie's. I'll fill you in when you get here. HH.* He rolled his eyes at Hailey signing off on a text message. He packed his hoodie and nightstick in the bag and made his way back over to Ollie's to meet with Hailey and see what had happened in the ten minutes since he had left.

"Over here, Locke!" Hailey shouted as he walked up. "He's with me," she said to the officer who stopped him as he walked up.

That officer and others were keeping people from getting too close to where the rest of the officers and Hailey were with the three attackers, the victim, and Ollie, who had come out of the bar just as the vigilante was running off.

"So, what happened?" Lance asked as he got next to Hailey.

"It appears that these three," she said, waving her pen in the direction of the attackers, "got into an argument with this man over here inside the bar as to which of their fraternities was the best. Then, they decided that the best way to settle the matter was with a three-on-one fight. Not long after they got the one guy to the ground, the vigilante showed up. He took the first of the three with two swings using some kind of stick, they said." She motioned her pen toward the attacker. "The guy never saw him coming. The second one rushed him, and they insist the vigilante kicked the guy in the chest with enough force to knock him into that wall"—she pointed to the bar—"which is most likely what Ollie heard. That's a lot of force." Lance nodded. "This is a small university, and I'm thinking that there's only a handful or two of guys on this campus who could get that much force behind a kick like that. A few of the athletes, maybe you or Jason, and you two really could have been athletes here, and maybe a few of the gym rats. I've already asked Jason, and he assures me he's not involved in the vigilantism, though he seemed worryingly disappointed by that fact. What about you, Locke? You secretly the guy in the hood?"

"Nope," Lance responded before fearing he had answered her too quickly.

Hailey seemed not to notice, though, as she continued.

"Exactly. So, there goes at least twenty percent of the people on campus that it could be. I'm going to start looking into some of the teams to see if I can get an idea of who this vigilante is. It would probably have to be a sport in the offseason. Maybe football?"

"Were they able to give any description of the guy?"

"Ha." Hailey rolled her eyes. "They each gave a description, but depending on which of the three you were talking to, you would be looking for either a stocky six-foot-tall man, an overweight six-foot-five guy, or someone who was 'at least six-foot-seven' that was 'thin as a rail.' So, nothing any more helpful than what Jessica gave us."

Lance had opened his mouth to respond when a young officer walked up.

"Do you have everything you need, Miss Hall?"

"Just about. I just had a couple of questions for the perpetrators."

"I'm afraid that won't be possible, ma'am," he told her. "They have each made it clear they won't be saying anything until they have an attorney present. I'm afraid that whether you have everything you need or not, you'll have to leave now."

"Can I at least have some names for my story?"

"The Gazette can request the police report with that information as soon as the report is filed, which should be sometime tomorrow morning. Until then, I am sorry, but there's nothing else I can do for you."

"I understand. Thank you, officer."

He lowered his head to her and walked Hailey and Lance back out of the crime scene.

"I guess I'll do what I can with the information I was able to get." She shrugged as they reached the sidewalk. "You need a ride back?"

"No, I know you're anxious to go write the story. I like walking back in the night air anyway. I'll see you tomorrow night." Lance waved as he headed back toward campus while Hailey walked the opposite direction to her car.

I guess I've answered the question on all of campus's mind, Lance thought to himself. *The vigilante is here to stay.*

chapter

THREE

A HERO'S ENCORE

Our new campus hero made another appearance last night, this time showing up outside of Ollie's bar to stop an assault from taking place. After three students had taken a fourth outside and had begun beating him, the vigilante showed up to prevent any more damage from being done. He fought the assaulters three-on-one, beating each of them before fleeing the scene when Ollie came to see what the noise coming from outside was. Officers on the scene claim that the victim, who had to be taken to the hospital for his injuries, was lucky the vigilante showed up when he did, or the injuries he sustained could have been much worse. We are all lucky to have someone looking out for our campus in this way. Thanking our mystery hero for the entire campus.

Hailey Hall

**The Franklin Gazette was unable to view the police report before going to print, so all updates to names and statuses will be posted in the digital version of this article.*

"Jason!" Lance bellowed from the living room, looking at his watch again, "Come on, man! We're already super late, and we're only going to this thing because of you!"

He tossed the newspaper back down on the table. He appreciated Hailey continuing to write about the vigilante in a positive light, but he was getting impatient waiting for her boyfriend.

"I swear, he takes longer to get ready than anyone I know," Taylor remarked to Lance, finishing just as Jason entered the room.

"You really think I'm that dumb? You expect me to think you two would be leaving your little sanctuary for anyone other than Gwen? Please. I mean, I get Lance doing it. Going to a party together is about as close as you can get to a date without actually having to admit your feelings. Still don't really know why you're going, though, Taylor."

"We're family!" Taylor cried, opening his eyes wide. "I should be in the clear more than Lance!"

"She's your cousin. That's barely blood," Jason answered, putting on his jacket and looking closely in the mirror. "Does my hair look alright?"

"You don't hardly have any hair. The little that you do have looks fine. And I'm sorry we can't all have four brothers to grow up with."

"Guys! I'm leaving. Okay?" Lance announced, interrupting their bickering, "If you want to walk, then be my guest, but we told Gwen and Hailey that we would pick them up fifteen minutes ago, so I'm heading over there before we end up being any later."

Jason and Taylor followed Lance out to his old truck, both hopping in the bed since he had only two seats in the cab. They left their apartment and arrived twenty minutes late at the girls' house. As Lance was still pulling to a stop in the drive, Jason hopped out of the bed and ran up to the door.

"You're thirty minutes late!" Lance and Taylor could hear Hailey's shout from the truck, even through the house door.

"Twenty!" Jason yelled back, scratching the back of his head.

Right then, the door opened. Hailey stormed out past Jason who ran after her trying to calm her down while Gwen locked the door behind them. Hailey and Jason got into the bed of the truck, where Hailey began talking to Taylor about medical school as she ignored Jason. Taylor, happy to aid in giving Jason the cold shoulder, jumped right into the conversation. Gwen climbed into the cab's passenger seat as Lance backed out of their driveway.

"Why didn't any of them sit up here? I would have sat in the back," Gwen said as she sat and looked over her shoulder at the conversation happening in the bed of Lance's truck, where Jason was still being ignored.

"I guess that at this point they just assume you have permanent shotgun when we're in my car," Lance chuckled as he backed out of their driveway.

"Oh."

They rode the short distance to the party in silence after that. As they pulled up to the house, Hailey, Jason, and Taylor all jumped out of the truck bed.

But before Lance could get out, Gwen asked, "Why do they think I have permanent shotgun?"

"Um. I, um, guess it's just because we've been best friends our whole lives. I don't really know. I haven't really thought about it before."

Before Gwen could say anything else, Taylor knocked on Gwen's window, pointing down and waiting for Gwen to crank the window down before speaking.

"There is not a chance I'm going in there without you two. I wouldn't even be here if you hadn't both asked me to come. Come on. Let's get this over with."

Lance didn't waste a second to get out of the car, opening the door for Gwen and putting the window back up before they all walked up to the house.

By the time Gwen, Lance, and Taylor entered the party, Hailey and Jason had disappeared into the crowd. Lance and Taylor followed Gwen as she made her way into a less crowded side room. They made their way to folding chairs that had been left earlier in the night, with the previous group having left a collection of cups and bottles littered around the chairs.

"I can't believe that I let the two of you talk me into coming to this," Taylor said as he tried to avoid as much of the litter as he could while he sat in the corner chair, brushing off crumbs before sitting on the edge of the seat.

"Well, if you hadn't come with me, I would be doing one of two things. I would either be sitting here by myself, having to convince people all night that, yes, I really am perfectly content just sitting by myself in silence and that, no, it really is unnecessary for them to try and adopt me as a friend for the night and sit here and force conversation with me instead of doing what they would otherwise do at a party. Or, worse yet, trying to follow Hailey and Jason from room to room all night, interacting with everyone they know, which, knowing them, is probably everyone who is here tonight," Gwen answered as she sat. "I really do appreciate you coming with me," she added with a smile to Taylor.

"You're welcome." Taylor sighed, leaning back in his chair and resigning himself to a night at the party. "What did you two think of Hailey's article today? The vigilante making his second appearance in a week to stop a mugging at Ollie's got her back on the front page."

"I was in the union studying last night when it happened," Lance told them, leaning forward in his chair. "I texted Hailey to see if she knew anything about it, and she invited me over to the scene. She didn't put it in her article, but it looks like it was some kind of frat fight. I guess that the three attackers decided that fighting the victim three-on-one was a good way to prove their fraternity's superiority. It sounded like the vigilante had gotten there just in time from what Hailey told me."

"Yeah, she said that the victim had almost been unconscious when the vigilante arrived. She said he couldn't remember anything about the vigilante's fight, just that he heard a bunch of noises, and they had stopped kicking him," Gwen added.

"So, it's beginning to look like this wasn't just a one-time act like some thought it might be," Taylor said. "It really does look like there's someone on our campus who is out there actively trying to protect the students."

"It looks like there is," Gwen agreed with a smile.

As midnight approached, and the party raged on, Gwen, Lance, and Taylor looked for Hailey and Jason to see if they could find a ride home. Gwen and Taylor both had homework they needed to do, and Lance claimed he wasn't feeling well. The three made it out to Lance's truck, where Taylor hopped back into the truck bed as Gwen took her seat in the cab. They dropped Gwen off and waited for her to get back in her house, then Lance and Taylor made their way back to their apartment. Taylor locked himself in his room to study while Lance prepared to go on his rounds for the night.

Lance was making his way to the library on his usual path when he saw two girls holding on to each other, stumbling toward the street separating the campus from the multitudes of apartment complexes that surrounded the area. Lance diverted and took a path to cut them off before they reached the road. He hadn't made it more than a few steps when one fell. The other helped her up and tried to stabilize her as they continued their walk to the apartments. Lance caught up as they approached the sidewalk and followed them from a short distance. When the two stumbled onto the road without paying any attention to the cars racing by in front of them, Lance sprinted into action.

As Lance left the curb, a car honked, and his heart skipped a beat. He saw the two girls standing in the street looking straight into the headlights, holding onto each other, frozen with wide eyes. Lance pushed himself into an all-out sprint to reach the girls before the car could. As the car was squealing to a stop, Lance successfully knocked the girls out of danger, getting himself clipped on the side by the car in the process. The impact sent him to the ground as the car tried to swerve to avoid hitting him. He clambered to his feet and hobbled back to the campus side of the road before the driver could get out and check on him.

Once he returned to the safety of the campus shadows' welcomed embrace, he climbed up the fire escape on the closest building to the first landing. He had rested there for a single breath before a couple of men walked underneath him, looking for the injured man who had just run from the road. Lance let out a sigh of relief as they made their way through the small corridor between the two buildings without looking up. He reached down to touch his hip and grimaced in pain, stifling a yelp. He slowly stood and looked out toward the street. The campus police had arrived and were questioning the two girls, the driver that had hit him, and the other cars that had seen what had happened and had stopped along the side of the road to see what they could do to help. Lance made his way further up the escape ladder with a pang of pain going through his entire right side each time that foot pushed off. After ten rungs, Lance had given up on pushing off with his right foot at all, and he used his left leg for each rung. When he had finally crawled onto the roof, Lance made his way to the edge where he could look out onto the road and waited for the scene below to clear out.

Forty-five minutes later, the last patrol car finally left the scene, and Lance made his way back to the fire escape. Still having to take it one rung at a time, now going down the ladder with his weight always on his left leg, Lance got to the ground at one-thirty. *There's no way I can keep going tonight,* he thought as he limped through the alley. *I'll see how I feel in the morning, and hopefully, I can try again tomorrow.* Lance limped his way through campus and the apartment parking lot, sticking to the shadows, praying no one saw the hobbled man dressed like the vigilante. He eventually made it back up to his apartment and unlocked the door, softly opening it to try not to make a sound. He had only taken a few steps in when he heard Jason's voice from the kitchen.

"I thought you were feeling sick." He was standing in their kitchen with his arms crossed. "Isn't that why you left the party early?"

"I thought getting some fresh air might help me," Lance answered with a shrug.

"It's almost two in the morning, Lance. I've been home for an hour and never saw you walk by. I don't believe for one second you were out getting some 'fresh air.'"

"Me either." Taylor's voice came from his room, soon followed by Taylor himself coming out.

"What have you been getting yourself into? We know this isn't the first time you've gone out this late at night. Contrary to what you seem to think, we aren't asleep by ten every night. We hear you leaving. You aren't that quiet."

"We also see you walking around looking exhausted all the time, like some sort of zombie. You're tired in class, you're tired at dinner, and you're tired when we're just hanging out watching TV. Really, Lance, what are you doing out this late?"

"I haven't been doing anything. I like walking around campus at night. And even if I was doing something, I don't need to listen to a lecture from either of you. You aren't my dad."

"We know that," Jason said. "That's the only reason we're still holding out hope you might listen to us."

"We're not trying to act like your dad, Lance. We're just worried about you. You've been out late a lot, and you're always tired. You weren't like this last semester or really any time before that either." Taylor paused as he looked over at Jason, who gave him a nod, before taking a deep breath and continuing, "You know you're not to blame for what happened to Gwen, right?"

"Don't. Don't talk to me about that again. You don't want to cross that line with me, Jansen."

"That's fine. Then, I'll take it from here," Jason said. "Taylor was trying to be gentle to avoid this conflict. He knows it's a sensitive subject for you, and he didn't want to upset you any more than necessary, but since that's clearly not working, I'll go ahead and shift gears. We know you blame yourself, Lance. It's obvious. It was obvious the night it happened, and it's been obvious every day since. That's not the question we're trying to answer. What we don't know is how you're coping besides going out at all hours of the night. You don't smell like alcohol. You don't seem to be on drugs. So, what in the world is going on with you, man? You're driving yourself insane, and this isn't helping Gwen. You know that, right? You know that you losing your mind and distancing yourself from everyone is causing her more pain than anything else could, don't you? You may not want to admit your feelings for her after what happened, but how she feels is clear. There's a reason you're the one who was listed as her emergency contact, Lance. Not her best friend and roommate. Not her cousin. Not her parents. You. You got the call for a reason. She isn't waiting for some knight in shining armor. She's waiting for you. But, honestly, for her sake, I hope that she stops waiting because, right now, you're in no shape—"

Lance's right fist connected with Jason's face as he stumbled backward to a knee.

Jason glared up at Lance as Taylor rushed to Jason, partially to help him back to his feet and partly to try and hold him back before things escalated any further. Lance stood above him for a moment, silent, fuming, before storming to his room with a limp and slamming the door behind him. He locked his door and threw his hoodie onto the bed, limping and grimacing as he paced around the room, cooling off.

Lance sat on the edge of his bed and stared at the wall. He pulled the nightstick from his hoodie and put it back in the box under his bed. He stood and stumbled into his bathroom to take ibuprofen for the pain in his hip. Laying down, he watched his ceiling fan rotate until the sunrise lit up the room. He rolled out of bed and walked to the gym without getting any sleep.

With his hip hurting, he couldn't work out like he had been for the last week. Jogging and lifting wouldn't be possible in his state, so he went to the aquatics center on the east end of the gym. Lowering himself into the cool water of the school's Olympic-sized pool, he walked a couple of laps to get the stiffness out of his right side. After he loosened up his injured hip, he swam laps, trying to do as much as he could without further injuring his hip.

While swimming, he made the decision to spend less time with Taylor and Jason. *The less they see of me, the less they will worry about me,* he thought to himself during his laps. It wouldn't be easy, and he would hate every part of it, but he knew when he had started his crusade that one thing that would come with protecting the campus would be him having to make sacrifices. He didn't realize his relationship with his two roommates and best friends would be that sacrifice, but it was worth it if it meant no one else had to suffer what Gwen did. And he would make sure that his mission succeeded.

FOUR

Lance began his rounds as he had every other night, walking toward the library, though this time, he was saddled with a limp. He passed by the library and continued on toward the union. He did a small fist pump when he got to the courtyard and found the balcony empty for the first time since he had stopped the attacker in the courtyard over a week ago. He took the fire escape ladder up, still wincing every time he pushed off his right leg, and settled in at the table. He hadn't seen Jason or Taylor since their argument last night, and he wasn't sure when he would see them again. With only months left before graduation, they would probably split ways soon enough, anyway. He could let them go off to Duncan, and he would go somewhere else. It's *not like there's a job waiting for me in Duncan,* he thought to himself. He could go anywhere he wanted. Duncan was the closest major city, but maybe he needed to get away from southwestern Missouri, at least for a bit. Maybe he would go to an East

Coast city like Sanders or Calvin. There were plenty of options to the west as well. He had always liked Colorado. Maybe Cameron City would be cool. Or go further west to the coast to some place in California. If he ever wanted to be adventurous and see what it would be like to live somewhere new, this was it.

Lance's thoughts were interrupted when a group of students walked into the courtyard. At first, he was afraid they were looking for the vigilante, but he breathed a sigh of relief when they stopped well short of the union. The group of seven guys stopped in the courtyard, waiting.

Lance crept from his seat to the balcony's edge, where he crouched to get a better look at the group. They all appeared to be students, and one of them held a briefcase, an odd sight at one-thirty in the morning. They stood nervously with their backs to each other, looking around as if they expected to be attacked at any moment and from any direction.

"Gentlemen."

The booming voice from the north end of the courtyard echoed off the walls around them as each student jumped, all quickly regrouping and turning to face the direction the voice had come from.

"I apologize for startling you," the smooth voice continued, softer but still firm, as a man emerged from the shadows. "That was never my intention." He finished with a wry smile.

Following the voice were three other men. One, who was holding a duffel bag, stood directly behind the man talking while the other two flanked the leader. The leader was taller than the rest of his entourage; he was at least an inch taller than Lance and looked to be in excellent shape. This second group appeared in stark contrast to the first. Where the students were dressed much like Lance in jeans and dark jackets, everyone in the second group were outfitted in suits. One of the students made his way out of the group to the man who had greeted them to meet him where he stood, five yards from where the students were standing.

They appeared to be in negotiation, but Lance couldn't hear much of what was being said, just gestures either to the man with the duffel bag or the student with the briefcase. Lance crept over to the fire escape and lightly tested it to ensure it wouldn't creak if he used it now. It didn't make a sound, so he slowly descended. Once he reached the ground, he made his way toward the meeting, sticking to the shadows until he reached a tree about twenty feet away from the conversation.

He settled in behind the tree as the lead student motioned forward the student holding the briefcase.

"So, here's what we've come up with at this point." The lead student motioned again to the student with the briefcase. "In this case,"—the student opened his briefcase to reveal a collection of glass vials, the speaker shifting his weight between both feet as he spoke—"we have one of the experimental drugs you requested. It has been quite difficult to create, even with the professor and our top students working on the project overtime. So far, we've only been able to create one of the drugs you've asked for. This," the student said, pulling a vial of blue liquid out of the briefcase, "is a chemical that will increase the strength of the body. It will work like a steroid in that it makes you stronger. But, unlike steroids, it won't make you grow, and you don't have to continue working out for it to work, though it will be exponentially beneficial to continue strengthening. This drug increases what the muscles can do at a micro level. How it works is that roughly every pound of muscle in someone using this will equal about four or five pounds of muscle for a normal human. So, where a person of normal strength could lift two hundred pounds, someone taking this drug could lift roughly one thousand pounds with the same output level. So, someone who is already able to lift four or five hundred pounds is now able to lift over two thousand. This drug also increases the skin's strength, making it less susceptible to being cut or bruised. We have also engineered it to increase the functioning of one's organs to prevent them from being overwhelmed by the body's new strength." He handed the vial to the man in the suit, who inspected the liquid before handing it back to the student. "So far, we've found injection works best in our trials. Pills have led to some nasty side effects and don't have the same increase in strength. Inhalants have increased strength even further but have a fatality rate far exceeding the additional strength gains."

The man in the lead of the second group nodded to the man with the duffel bag, who walked forward. The man dropped the duffel bag in front of the students and retrieved the briefcase. The man returned to his place with the briefcase in hand as the students rejoined their group.

"This should cover the cost of what you brought tonight. I assume you have more of my requested drugs in your warehouse?"

"We do."

"Excellent. Can you have me two cases of vials for these drugs by tomorrow night?"

"We don't have that much inventory in our warehouse." The student responded, looking down and rubbing the back of his head. He shifted his weight from one leg to another and back again before making eye contact. "We've just recently found the correct formula and only had enough materials left to make a small batch of this. We can have half of a case by tomorrow, but getting you what you're asking for will take at least four to six weeks. The professor has already put an order in for the missing ingredients."

"Fine. Then, we will meet again tomorrow to exchange what you have and supply you with whatever you need to create more. I think that's all we need to cover for now." He looked at each of his associates, who each nodded, then turned back to the lead student. "We will meet you here at the same time tomorrow."

With that, all four suited men turned and made their way toward the shadows at the north end of the courtyard.

The lead student picked up the duffel bag and followed the rest of his group away from the courtyard. Lance followed from a safe distance, avoiding the lit pathway. He kept up with them for a short distance, but a large group of students came out as they neared the library. Lance looked at his watch to see that it was two in the morning, meaning the library had just closed. Pinned against the side of a building to keep from being seen, Lance lost sight of the group from the courtyard. Once the students cleared out and Lance could leave the shadows, the group had vanished. He started back to the apartment. Those weren't just drugs being dealt. This was something bigger. This was a weapon. But who could have the resources to fund this experimentation? And why use a college campus and college students to do it?

Lance stuck to the shadows as he walked home, looking for other incidents around campus. He found none. He snuck through the parking lot and up the stairs to his floor. He held his breath as the door swung open, but all the lights were out. No ambush was waiting for him tonight. He closed his door behind him and collapsed onto the bed. He slid the nightstick out of his pocket and lowered it to the floor. He rubbed his hip, still sore from the night before, then carefully rolled from his back to his stomach, reaching down to push the weapon under his bed before rolling again to his back for the night, staring at the ceiling until the room lightened with the sunrise.

Lance limped into the cafeteria after his second sleepless night in as many days and headed straight for the breakfast bar. After loading his plate up with waffles, eggs, and bacon, he looked for an open table. He found one tucked in a corner and ate his breakfast alone, the greasy and sugary foods helping to ease his exhaustion. After ten minutes of eating, Gwen found him and sat across the table.

"Are you okay, Lance?" she asked bluntly, skipping any pleasantries, which was out of character for her.

Lance took his time to finish chewing his food before answering. "Never better. Why?"

"Because"—she took a deep breath and then rushed forward like she was trying to get what she had to say over with as soon as possible—"you've been acting differently. Jason and Taylor told us about what happened the other night when you guys got into your fight. They wanted to know if we had any idea what had gotten into you. I told them I had talked to you and that you said that you were fine, but they didn't believe that any more than I did. You know that I hate this, but I'm really worried about you. What's wrong, Lance?"

"I already told you," he answered, laying his fork down, "I'm just a little stressed out about what I'm going to do after graduation. Taylor has already been accepted into Duncan's medical school, and Jason already has an offer from the engineering branch of Fox Industries. Hailey has three journalism offers, and you're having your social work internship converted into a new position this summer. I'm the only one without a plan, and I'm stressing out about it. Don't get me wrong, I'm happy for all of you, but it's also frustrating seeing everyone else figuring it out while I have no idea what I am going to do with my life or what the point has been of everything I've done up until this point, you know? That's all it is. I know it seems foreign to the rest of you to not have my future figured out already, but this is what it looks like."

"Lance, you look like you haven't slept in a week. It's getting worse."

"I told you I'm fine."

"So, none of this has anything to do with you blaming yourself for what happened to me that night walking back from the library?"

Lance looked down at his food in silence. He stabbed his eggs with his fork, but he just set the fork back down without eating them. He had lost his appetite. After what felt like an eternity for Lance, Gwen took his silence as an answer and continued.

"It does, doesn't it? They were right," she said, shaking her head in a mixture of disbelief and sadness. "Last night, they said that they thought that was what was wrong with you. I couldn't believe they could think that. There was no way you could blame yourself. You had nothing to do with it, and you did nothing wrong. But they were right. It is my fault that you're acting like this," she said, the last line almost a whisper, her eyes gleaming as she stared into Lance's.

"No. None of this is your fault. Everything would be the same if I had just gone to study with you that night. But I didn't. I wanted to be alone, and as a result—"

"No!" Gwen exclaimed, causing the table next to them to jump and look over at them as she continued. "There's no 'as a result,' Lance. You studying by yourself did not sentence me to be assaulted walking home from the library. Stop pitying yourself. You're the one preventing us from getting back to normal. That's all I want. I don't want you to feel guilty, or to pity me, or to blame yourself for something that happened that was beyond yours or mine or anyone else's control. None of that helps anyone. All I want is for us to be normal again."

Gwen abruptly stood and picked up the dishes with her barely touched food still on them. She avoided looking up at Lance as she gathered them. And when she had finally finished collecting her things and spoke, there was a tear in her eye, but her voice was steady as she looked at Lance.

"If you really feel this strongly about this all being your fault, then spending time with me is probably only causing you more grief. Until you can figure this out, figure out how to forgive yourself, it's probably for the best that we don't see each other as much. Taylor's birthday isn't too far away, so I guess I'll see you then. Goodbye, Lance."

She walked away without looking back as he sat there in stunned silence watching her put her plate on the shelf and leave through the doors into the bright morning light.

chapter

FIVE

Taylor pulled into the apartment complex's parking lot at one-fifteen a.m. and pressed the base of his palms into both eyes as he let out a long sigh. He had been at a friend's house studying with a group from his neurobiology class and was not looking forward to his test in that class at eight the following morning. In four years of classes, this was the first course that had him feeling out of his depth. He was still confident he could pull out an A and another four-point-oh GPA by the end of the semester, but it wouldn't be as effortless as it had been for his other terms leading up to now.

He turned off his car and reached over to grab his backpack when he saw someone walking across the parking lot in front of him. The person was wearing dark pants and a dark hoodie so that he couldn't be positive, but it looked like Lance. Taylor looked at his watch and sighed again before getting out of his car and following the man.

The man was already across the street separating the apartments from campus by the time Taylor had gotten out of his car. Taylor jogged across the street but slowed down once he was on the campus sidewalk. He tried catching up to the man, walking as fast as possible up the sidewalk without looking suspicious, but he kept losing him in the shadows. It didn't help that Taylor didn't want to spook whoever he was following by constantly staring into the shadows, so he would only let himself look to the sides where he thought the man should be every so often. If it was Lance, letting himself be heard would lead to another lie from Lance about what he was doing and how it wasn't what it looked like.

Not that Taylor was even sure what this looked like to begin with. No, the only way he'd be able to figure out what Lance had been getting up to was by catching up to him and seeing him do it without being heard. And if it wasn't Lance? Well, he would still rather not be seen because whoever this was had some reason for not wanting to be followed, and Taylor didn't want to know what they would do if they found out they had failed. He pulled his phone out of his pocket just in case. He'd feel safer knowing his ability to call for help was that much easier if anything went wrong.

If this is Lance, Taylor thought, having slowed his walk, *what could he possibly be doing out here this late at night? Does he just wander around the campus, sticking to the shadows?*

Is this some sort of coping mechanism for his grief? His guilt? Taylor understood how he must feel. He had also told Gwen he didn't want to study that night. He also could have potentially protected her from what had happened if he had only been there. But what happened wasn't his fault, and he understood that, as much as he regretted what had happened and thought of what could have gone differently, he knew it wasn't on him. And he knew it wasn't on Lance, either. Gwen felt the same way.

He knew she felt that way because he had taken the time to actually talk with her about it. Both he and Gwen were only children. With his father having no siblings and Gwen's father's family all being out of state, they were close cousins, almost sibling-like in their relationship. Being roughly the same age, she was a couple of months older than him, and from nearby towns, they had been inseparable growing up. Lance would often tag along, being another only child and Gwen's best friend. They had talked about everything under the sun, it seemed to him, but this conversation was the toughest for him to have with her. It was also the most important.

He had shared his guilt and regret with her, apologizing for not being there when she needed him most. And she assured him, through her own tears, that he wasn't to blame and that there was nothing he needed to be forgiven of. It had not been an easy journey, but through talking with Gwen and his counselor, Taylor put behind his guilt from that night and accepted that it wasn't his fault. As much as he tried convincing Lance to have those same conversations, he hadn't had any luck.

Taylor had about given up all hope of finding the person in the shadows when the mystery figure finally cut back across the sidewalk and into the union courtyard. Taylor followed from a distance, listening closely and walking slowly, trying to hide in the shadows that the man had just left, watching as the man climbed the tree in the center of the courtyard. The mystery man seemed to struggle for a second to push off his right leg but got his left leg onto a branch and worked his way up, though he continued to hesitate each time he would have to push off his right leg to climb up to another branch.

Taylor slid his phone back into his pocket and inched closer to get a better look. As the man climbed higher into the tree, Taylor finally recognized something concrete to confirm his suspicions, something he had been looking for this whole time.

The shoes. The shoes that he saw left in his entryway every night. The shoes coming apart just ever so slightly at the heel. The shoes. They were unmistakably Lance's. Taylor slowly backed away until he was in the cover of the shadows and then turned back toward the apartment and began to jog. After a few yards, he pulled his phone back out of his pocket and called Jason. He put the phone to his ear as he jogged, listening to the line ringing as he waited.

"Jason," he began when Jason picked up, not giving his friend the chance to say a word, "you are not going to believe what I just saw. Are you still dressed? Well, put your shoes back on. I need you to come check something out. You're going to want to see this."

SIX

Lance made himself as comfortable as he could in the courtyard's tree, which, with his hip hurting even more that night than it had previously, wasn't very comfortable. But from this position, he could see and hear what was happening below without being spotted. The vantage point was worth the extra discomfort, or at least that's what he told himself to make the whole thing bearable.

He showed up ten minutes early for the meeting to ensure he wouldn't be seen climbing into the tree by the meeting's parties. He wasn't as early as he thought, though, for barely a minute had passed before the students appeared together from the corridor in front of the library that Lance had also come from, their briefcase in tow.

The group stood in silence as they waited in the chilly night, again with their backs to one another so they could see each direction. There were fewer students tonight, Lance noticed. This time, there were only four. To match the number of the more professional group they were dealing with had brought, he assumed. They still wore their jeans and hoodies, but the smaller number made them look less conspicuous. Had he been on a typical night of patrol, he likely would have thought nothing of this group in the courtyard like he had of their larger group the night before.

The student who had handled the talking at the previous meeting was there again, but Lance couldn't tell if the others had also been there the previous night. He fidgeted and looked down at his watch every thirty seconds, trying to stay quiet. Lance was looking at his watch right as the hands turned to one-thirty.

Before he could look back up from his wrist, he heard "gentlemen" from across the courtyard, perfectly on time for the meeting. Lance jumped as the voice broke through the silent night. The branches he was in creaked and swayed as he moved. He held his breath and silently cursed himself, praying the movement wouldn't give away his position. Luckily for Lance, the students had also been startled by the man's voice and were too preoccupied with their own shuffling to notice the tree's movements.

They settled down as the other group approached. This group, Lance noticed, was the same that had been present the night before. The four of them came to a stop in front of the students. The only difference between tonight's group and last night's was that they came carrying two duffel bags to the students' one briefcase this time.

"Mr. Fox." The lead student greeted the man in front, stepping forward to meet him after having composed himself after Fox had startled him with his arrival. "We have brought all that remained of our supply as you asked. In this case, you will find twenty vials of the special drug you requested. The professor is working with a group as we speak to fill the rest of your order by your deadline."

"And you," the man he called Fox responded, smiling, and motioning the men with bags forward, "will find fifty thousand dollars in each of these duffel bags."

Lance's jaw dropped after hearing the amount of money switching hands. *One hundred thousand dollars!* He wasn't alone in his shock either. The lead student opened his eyes wider after hearing his payday, while the other students all squirmed while trying to maintain composure. The leader quickly returned to his straight face, but not before Fox smirked to let him know he saw the reaction.

"One of the bags should cover this transaction, while the other should hold you over until you have more for me."

The two men, now without their duffel bags, fell back into place around Mr. Fox as the third retrieved the briefcase from the students. He unlatched the case and opened it to show Fox. Lance could just barely make out the blue vials inside. Even in the dark courtyard, Lance could see a faint blue light emanating from the briefcase as the vials reflected the little light available to them. Pleased with the contents, Fox nodded to his lackey, who abruptly shut the case and stationed himself back in his place directly behind Fox.

"That's very generous of you, Mr. Fox. We weren't expecting the second bag tonight," the lead student said, finally regaining his composure enough to talk.

As he said this, two students picked up the duffel bags and backed into their spots without opening either bag.

"I treat my employees very well," he said before gesturing to the students with a smile, "and my partners even better. Now, this payment is not without any expectations. I want my next batch finished no later than one month from today. I don't care what must happen for that to get done; just have the professor see to it that it does. You know how to reach me if I can assist you. I believe this is all the business we have to cover at the time being. Unless you have anything else to add, I believe we will be on our way. Good night, then, gentlemen."

Fox gave the students a curt nod and then, without giving them time to add anything, had they wanted to, turned, and followed his men back out of the courtyard as they had entered earlier.

The students stayed where they were as they watched the group leave the courtyard. When the last of the group was out of sight, though, they all rifled through the duffel bags. They did not have time to count it all there. There were far too many bills for that, and none of the students had seen one hundred thousand dollars before, but they all agreed that in these bags was an enormous amount of money. They zipped the bags and walked quickly home.

After they exited the courtyard, Lance dropped himself from the tree as quietly as he could and followed them from the shadows, nightstick drawn. He had not followed long, though, before he stepped on one of the countless acorns that littered the campus that had rolled onto the sidewalk, resulting in a loud crunch.

The students froze. Lance, realizing the element of surprise would be with him for only a second more, immediately lurched forward and launched a preemptive attack before they turned toward him. He struck the student in the tail of the group in the back with the nightstick before moving to the student on his left. He kicked this student in the knee as a yelp leaped from the student's lips. Lance turned back toward the group as the other three moved in on him. They had let the duffel bags fall to the ground as they turned their full attention to him.

Lance struck first again before they dictated the fight. He attacked the one on the furthest right, the same one he had hit across the back. He struck him in the arm and on the hip before the student connected with a blow to Lance's chest. Lance staggered backward and waited there for the student to rush him again, which he did immediately. Lance crouched into a stance before sweeping his leg as the student rushed him. He raised his arm and hit him across the chest with his nightstick as the student fell to the ground.

Lance looked up to find it was once again three against one as the student he had kicked in the leg was, while hobbled, back standing with the others. The two he hadn't engaged yet rushed him at the same time. They both connected with a flurry of punches as Lance raised his left arm and tried to protect himself. He caught one student in the hip with his nightstick and escaped past him in the momentary lull as the student grabbed for his side.

He wasn't away long enough to even catch a couple of breaths, though, before the third student came at him. Lance connected with a mixture of punches and hits with his nightstick, culminating in another blow to the student's knee that he had hit earlier during the fight, sending the student sprawling to the ground. He finished with one last strike with the nightstick to his head as the student's body went limp against the sidewalk.

Lance found himself again in a two-on-one situation, though, as the two remaining students had returned to where he was. Lance tried to split them up and fight them, each one at a time, but each time he would get one of them away from the other, he would almost instantly get hit from behind as the other rejoined the fight. He had gotten a few hits in with the nightstick on each of them, but he was taking a much bigger beating than he was dealing out.

He panted as he leaped backward after connecting on a combination of hits, sweat dripping down out of his matted hair down onto his nose. He tried to jump back into the fray by swinging his nightstick at the lead student's ribs, but the student deflected the fatigued swing and sent Lance's nightstick clattering to a stop on the sidewalk.

The three stood silently as they all watched the nightstick slowly roll to a stop. Lance gulped as he tried to steady himself for the onslaught he knew was coming, but it didn't make a difference. After losing his nightstick, Lance went from getting beat to being beaten quickly.

Without his nightstick, the two-on-one advantage became even more prominent as they no longer had to fear his weapon. He connected with body punches before being forced to jump back in retreat as they overpowered him again. He tried to connect with enough punches to buy himself the space to jump back and retreat again, trying to prolong the fight until something could distract the two students enough for him to escape or for another student to show up and stop the fight somehow. He had given up the idea of winning the fight and only held on to the hope that he could *endure* long enough to keep from being overwhelmed.

That hope only lasted moments longer. He had jumped back in retreat once more after a flurry of punches as he had done twice, but this time, his foot struck one of the fallen students as he landed, and his ankle gave way as he fell to the ground. The two students immediately pounced on him as he landed, and once the three were all on the ground, the two students traded off punches as he lay there helpless. The sides of his vision darkened as the punches continued to land on his body and head.

Lance lost consciousness right as the two stopped hitting him. He felt their weight leave him as he heard them rush to grab the bags and their two partners Lance had knocked out earlier, leaving Lance lying on the ground unmoving. Lance faintly heard his name being called and saw two people rushing up to him as he blacked out.

SEVEN

"Lance!" Jason yelled, sprinting up to him and shaking his shoulders as Lance's head swayed limply.

Jason had been sitting on their couch in the living room reading yet another article for class when he got Taylor's call. He had been out for a date night with Hailey and hadn't had time to take care of his reading beforehand, so he was catching up before his test the next day. He needed to focus and finish that reading, but he could tell by the tone in Taylor's voice this was something important, so he reluctantly put his shoes back on. He grabbed his jacket off the top of the couch, locked the door to the apartment, and made his way down the stairs to see where Taylor was trying to drag him at one-thirty in the morning.

Taylor got to the apartment a minute after Jason had come down and found him sitting at the bottom of the stairwell. He was still panting from jogging all the way back from the courtyard, but he beckoned for Jason to follow him back the way he had come as he tried to catch his breath. As they walked, Taylor filled Jason in on what he saw when he got back to the apartment, why he had followed, and what he had seen to make him realize that it was Lance. Taylor had just explained the situation when they heard a shout coming from just outside the courtyard before Jason could ask any follow-up questions. They saw a handful of people moving around in the distance, and then someone fell to the ground while everyone else continued fighting. They broke into a sprint, Jason considerably outpacing Taylor as they tried to reach Lance. Another person fell, and Jason redoubled his pace. This time, the fight followed the man who had fallen to the ground, with the two remaining fighters jumping on top and taking turns throwing punches. Jason gave a shout that caused the two fighters to stand up, grab a couple of bags, and pull away two others before Jason could get there.

Seconds later, Jason made it to the person who had been left behind. The hood had fallen off during the fight, but even then, it took Jason a moment to figure out it was Lance. His face was severely swollen, cut, and splotched four colors. A lump formed in Jason's throat as he looked down at his friend.

"What has he gotten himself into?" Jason whispered.

"I think," Taylor said, having stopped where Lance's nightstick had fallen, "this might be your answer." He picked it up and walked it to Jason.

"What does that mean?" he asked in a hollow voice, taking the nightstick and rotating it in his hands several times over as though it would unlock the secrets Lance had been keeping from them if only he looked hard enough.

"It means that we were right. And that we were wrong. Lance has definitely been more affected by what happened to Gwen than he had been letting on, but he wasn't just walking around the campus moping about it. He's been walking around the campus fighting. The vigilante appearing right after what happened to Gwen no longer appears to be the coincidence we thought it was. It's Lance. He's the vigilante."

"You take this," Jason said, handing the nightstick back to Taylor, urgency and decisiveness in his voice now, "and I'll carry him. We have to get him back up to the apartment as fast as we can. These wounds probably need to be treated as soon as possible; don't you think? Do you still have any of those old medical kits back at the apartment?"

"Yeah, I actually do. I still have a couple up in my room," Taylor responded.

"Good. Because it looks like you've got yourself a new patient, Doctor Jansen," Jason said as he lifted Lance into his arms in a fireman's carry and walked back to their apartment at as constant speed as he could manage.

Even weighed down by Lance, they made good time crossing campus as Jason's adrenaline pushed him to get Lance to safety quickly. Barely five minutes had passed before they reached the apartment steps, and Taylor took off ahead of Jason and Lance, fumbling with his keys for the lock.

Taylor threw the door to their apartment open and Jason rushed through behind him with Lance still cradled in his arms. Taylor disappeared into his room while the door was still shutting behind Jason. While Taylor ran to his room, Jason gently laid Lance on the sofa. Taylor hurried back out carrying one of his medical kits.

"What all do you think is wrong with him?" Jason asked, scratching his head as Taylor reentered the living room and set up his equipment next to the couch.

"Hopefully, just some bruises and cuts. I mean, on top of the fact that he's clearly unconscious and has a concussion. Here, help me get his shirt off."

They gingerly took off his hoodie, but his shirt clung to his body where blood and sweat met the fabric. Rather than risk worsening his wounds by yanking the shirt off, Taylor decided to just cut it off with a pair of scissors from his kit. Once they had cut a line up each side and then across the sleeves, they removed what was left of his shirt, though they still had to be careful as the shirt was still sticking stubbornly to the blood and sweat around his wounds.

What they found under the shirt was an awful sight. Lance had large bruises down each arm and across his chest and abdomen. The worst bruise, though, was a purple number that started somewhere below the pant line on his right leg and continued through his hip and on up his side, at least a foot wide at its widest. The skin on this one was already soft and mushy, and an odor was coming up from it.

"Oh," Jason muttered, turning from the site. He took a deep breath and swallowed before clenching his jaw and turning back to Taylor. "What do you need me to do?"

"We're going to need a whole lot of ice. Go and fill a couple of larger bags for his torso and several smaller ones for his arms and head. I'm also going to need a small bowl of warm water and a dish towel to clean his wounds. Bring the bowl of water first so I can work to clean some of this away before we ice him."

As Jason went into the kitchen to start working on what he had asked for, Taylor moved on to Lance's face. There were more bruises and a couple of knots already beginning to form on his forehead, but there was nothing Taylor could do about those until Jason came back in with the ice, so he started with the cuts.

Jason came back in with the warm water and turned to go back and prepare the ice before Taylor stopped him.

"I need you to lift him up so I can get the rest of his shirt off him."

Jason gently lifted Lance's torso off the couch and Taylor pulled what was left of the shirt off. Jason went back after the ice without another word as Taylor returned his attention to Lance's face. Most cuts required nothing more than cleaning and bandaging, but that would not be enough for an especially deep gash across his chin.

"Where are you going?" Jason asked as Taylor left the room right as he came in with the ice.

"I need a different kit. He needs a few stitches on his chin."

"And you don't think we should take him to someone who has at least started medical school to get that done?" hollered Jason toward Taylor's room.

"Please," Taylor answered, coming back into the living room with the new kit, "Stitches are simple. It's just sewing. Plus, I don't think he would take kindly to us giving up his secret so soon after we learned it. Have you never read a comic book? Also, don't you think there was probably a reason he hadn't told us he was the vigilante? This isn't our secret to reveal. Besides, I've stitched up animals before, which shouldn't be too different. Now, hold his head steady while I do this."

Neither spoke while Taylor worked. His grandma had taught him how to sew when he was a child. He had fond memories of helping her create quilts and sweaters growing up. His father had looked down on it when he started the hobby and came around only when he realized that the steady hands sewing created would serve him well when he became a doctor. That's what it always seemed to come back to. With just three stitches needed, Taylor finished quickly with little trouble.

"Is he going to be okay?"

"I think so. Most of his injuries weren't too bad, though I am a little worried about his hip. He should be quite a bit better in the morning, but it will probably take a few days for him to actually feel good again."

"And what do you think about finding out that it's been him who was the vigilante this whole time? You seem pretty calm about the whole thing."

"I haven't really been thinking about it. Hand me that big pack of ice. My first concern was making sure he was okay, so I've been a bit preoccupied. Now that he's been treated, I guess I'm not sure how to feel." Taylor wrapped the ice to Lance's hip with some gauze. "I guess this explains his strange behavior. Sneaking out late at night, being secretive and tired all the time. Hand me some smaller bags for his arms. Those all line up with this, I guess. It also makes sense with how he's felt about what happened to Gwen. Him wanting to go out and protect the campus after that seems pretty on brand for him and a reasonable response to that grief."

"Reasonable? *Reasonable*? That's the word you're going to go with here? Taylor, he's been running around campus in the dark with his nightstick, fighting whoever he comes across for who knows how long!" Jason shouted before lowering his voice down to a normal level. "In no way is any of this reasonable, Taylor. Yes, I guess it makes some sort of sense with what he went through with Gwen, but this is in no way reasonable. This is insane. This is the opposite of reasonable. We have to tell Hailey and Gwen."

"No chance. First off, Lance didn't want us to know, so there's no way he's going to want Hailey or Gwen, especially Gwen, to know what he's been up to at night—another small bag for his face. Hailey would want to let everyone know who has been protecting the campus in the paper. She would feel it was her journalistic duty and probably even think it was only fair that Lance gets the recognition he deserves. But have you met Lance? That attention would mortify him. And Gwen—well, we would be the ones getting beaten with that nightstick of his if we so much as entertained the thought of telling Gwen. He's doing this for her; if she knew that, she would probably hate herself." He turned to look at Lance on the couch and finished in a whisper. "Especially if she could see him now."

"So, what do you suggest we do?" Jason asked, throwing his hands on top of his head. "We just continue on as if we don't know?" His hands came back down to gesture at Lance. "Let him go crazy on any person he decides is bad that's running around campus at night?"

"Wait until he wakes up." Taylor finally answered after getting the ice to sit on Lance's face just right. "Let's give him a chance to explain himself before we do anything. I don't think we can act like we don't know now, not after finding him like this with his nightstick beside him; it's clear what he's been doing. We'll have to let him know that we know, but whatever comes next, he should at least have a say in."

Jason looked from Taylor to Lance and back again before nodding.

"You're right. We'll give him a chance to explain. But man. This is going to take a lot of explaining." He took a deep breath, exhaling out of his mouth as he tilted his head back and headed for his room, calling out over his shoulder, "Night, man."

After hearing Jason's bedroom door close, Taylor curled up in the chair directly across from the couch and fell asleep there.

EIGHT

Lance woke as light filled the room. He stared blankly up at the ceiling fan, blinking repeatedly to try and clear the fog clouding his mind. He knew he was back in the apartment but had no idea how he could have gotten there. He tried to focus on one of the fan's blades as it went around but couldn't focus long enough to watch it make a single rotation. He attempted to sit up to get his bearings.

"Ughh."

A hoarse groan jumped from his lips as his body convulsed, and he slammed back down onto the couch, panting. Every inch of his body burned as he lay back down, trying to regulate his breathing. He shook as the aftershocks from his pain traveled through his body.

"Lance don't try to move right now," Taylor said. "We were able to get the swelling down, but there wasn't much we could do for the pain while you were unconscious. Now that you're up, I can get you some pain medicine."

Taylor rushed back into his room, almost running into Jason, who was lumbering from his room, awakened by Lance's groan. Taylor came back and put the painkillers in Lance's mouth and then gave him a drink of water to help him swallow while Jason reapplied the ice bags. They sat in silence as Lance got used to the ice.

"What happened?" he finally asked.

Jason and Taylor looked at one another, trying to figure out where to start.

After the pause, Taylor answered, "I saw you leaving the apartment last night when I got home from studying. I followed you across campus, and once I saw you climb the tree, I came back to get Jason. Then we headed back to the courtyard to look for you. We were almost there when we heard someone yell, and then what sounded like fighting. By the time we got there, you had taken out two of the four, but the other two were on top of you, taking turns punching. Once Jason yelled and ran up, they grabbed their bags and the two you had taken out and left."

"I wanted to chase after them, but with the shape you were in, we knew that we had to get you back here as soon as we could."

"Jason carried you back, and then I cleaned and bandaged your cuts, stitched up your chin, and began icing your injuries to keep it from swelling."

Lance slowly reached up to feel the stitches. "I was just out for a walk when those guys jumped me. I never saw it coming. Guess the vigilante can't stop everything going on around here. The campus is just too—"

"Cut the crap, Lance. We know you're him; we know you're the vigilante. Taylor found your nightstick not far from where you had been fighting. Why didn't you tell us?" Jason asked.

Taylor shot Jason an angry look before leaning back against the chair with a sigh. Taylor had wanted to ease into this confrontation, especially considering the shape Lance was in, but he couldn't blame Jason for wanting answers from Lance. He wanted them, too.

"I have no idea what you're talking about," Lance responded, avoiding looking at Jason by staring straight up at the ceiling fan instead, trying again to focus on a single blade's rotation with no more luck than he had during his first attempt.

"Are you kidding me, Lance? You're covered in bruises, one of which Taylor said definitely didn't come from last night, and you've been going on walks every night with your dad's old nightstick. And you're going to sit there and tell me you weren't out there looking for people to fight? You expect me to believe that?"

"That's exactly what I'm telling you."

"You two can argue about Lance's extracurriculars and if he is or isn't the vigilante later," Taylor cut in, leaning up in his chair and raising his voice. "What I need to know right now, though, is how long ago you got that bruise on your hip. If we don't get that taken care of soon, you could be in some serious trouble."

"It happened a few days ago."

"Let me guess. You were just on a nice nighttime stroll across campus when, all of a sudden, a car hit you?" Jason said, pacing between Lance and Taylor.

"More or less."

"You got hit by a car?" Jason shouted, his pacing stopping abruptly. "And you still expect me to believe that you're not doing anything but taking leisurely walks? Why in the world would you not tell us that you had been hit by a car if there wasn't something you were trying to hide?"

"Guys," Taylor tried to calm them down.

"Well, I was going to tell you, but when I got back that night, you two decided to stage your little intervention. I didn't really feel like telling either of you much of anything after that. I certainly wasn't going to be asking for your help then."

"And can you blame us for thinking you needed an intervention after you were going around jumping in front of cars and fighting people across campus?"

"Guys!" Taylor tried again.

"I thought after four years, maybe I had earned some trust. That you would maybe give me the benefit of the doubt, that I would be willing to give you." Lance was now shouting back at Jason, leaning up as an ice pack fell off him.

"Well, you've done a pretty good job of undercutting that in the three months since Gwen—"

"GUYS!"

Lance and Jason fell silent and turned to Taylor to see all five-foot-nine of him fuming. They weren't sure if it was their bickering, Lance getting so worked up with his injuries, or Jason bringing up Gwen, but for the first time in either of their lives, they were both legitimately afraid of Taylor Jansen as he stood above them.

"Lance, you want to yell about having earned our trust. Well, we've earned yours, too. You're not the only one who cares about protecting this campus or Gwen, and you're not the only one who chose to study alone that night over going with her to the library. She invited me, too. I'm the one she's related to. She's basically my sister. I have just as much of a reason to feel guilty and upset as you do. And Jason, do you really think that screaming at him will solve anything? He was clearly worried about how we would respond if we found out what he had been doing and, judging by your reaction, I'm thinking that keeping it from us was a pretty smart call. And if you want to say anything else about Gwen, I would suggest looking for a new place to live. I'm the one with the name on the lease, and I'm the one paying for both of your rent. If I were you, I would think twice before saying anything else about my cousin. Now"— he sat back down and took a deep breath to compose himself—"Lance, I'm not sure what Jason wants to do, but I'm in."

"I'm in, too," Jason immediately answered.

"Wait, what do you mean you're in?"

"I mean, whatever I can do to help, I will. You want to protect this campus? Well, so do I. From the look of this," he said, gesturing to Lance lying on the couch, "you're going to need all the help you can get."

"This must be stronger pain medication than I realized. Absolutely not. I may not be as big and strong as Jason or as smart as you, but if my lunatic father prepared me for anything with all of the fighting classes and cop training bull crap he put me through, it was to protect people. And part of that means not bringing extra people into the crossfire."

"Do we need to remind you where we just rescued you from?" Jason asked incredulously. "I may not have all of your technical training, but growing up with four older brothers, I know a thing or two about fighting. And," he said, breaking into a large smile, "that's not even the biggest skill I bring to the table. And Taylor may not be much of a fighter, but you wouldn't be either anytime soon if he hadn't been able to take care of you last night. We're not children who need protecting."

"Jason's right, Lance. We may not possess the same skills that make you a good vigilante, but we do have the skills that would turn you into a great one. If you truly want to protect this campus, you'll let us help."

"I'll think about it. For now, you two have classes, and I need to shower and lie back down. We can talk about it again this evening," he said, taking off his ice bags and placing them in the kitchen, limping as he headed for his room.

Jason turned to Taylor once he was gone, "We're not really going to wait until we talk to him again this evening to get started helping him, are we?"

"Not a chance. Meet me after you're through with class today. I have a few ideas," Taylor answered with a smile as he cleaned and packed away the medical supplies he had left out just in case.

"That's what I was hoping you were going to say," Jason said as a grin broke across his face.

While Taylor continued putting his kit back together, Jason walked back to his room to get ready for his classes.

NINE

Lance turned the knob of the apartment's front door and softly pulled it to a close to keep it from making any noise. He stepped out into the flickering lights of the concrete hall at one in the morning and hadn't seen Taylor or Jason since he took a nap after dinner. He tip-toed away from the door and hurriedly hobbled down the stairs. He froze halfway down the last flight when he found Jason and Taylor sitting on the bottom steps, waiting for him.

"We figured you'd try to go out again tonight," Jason said as he and Taylor stood and turned to face Lance. "You really aren't that bright, are you?"

"Seriously, Lance, I'm still not convinced you don't need X-rays. But broken bones or not, I am convinced that you don't need to be doing your vigilantism for at least the next couple of nights. And you should probably take at least a full week off to fully heal."

"I have to go. Part of protecting the campus is making sure people know there is someone out there every night," he said, jabbing his hand toward campus. "Even if I don't stop someone, people knowing I'm out there makes them feel safer. Everyone wants to feel like they have someone watching over them and protecting them. If I take the night off and something happens, that feeling will be lost, and the sense of security I've built up for them will be gone. They won't know if they are being protected anymore. I have to go."

"I understand what you're saying, and honestly, you might even be right, but you can't protect anyone with the condition you're in. Take Jason with you. There will be people out on the campus, and he can handle any conflict that comes up."

"Nope. No way. I'm still not sure if either of you should be involved at all. I definitely don't feel comfortable throwing Jason into the fire like this the day after he's learned about it. Besides, I prefer to work solo."

"Yeah, sorry, Lance, but this isn't something you have much say about in your condition. Taylor's right. The only way you're going is with me by your side. You'll have the final say on what I get involved in, but if a conflict comes up, I'm going to be the one doing the fighting. Face it, if something does happen tonight, and you can't prevent it due to the shape you're in, the fallout will be the same as far as the security of the campus goes, maybe even worse if people find out you can be beat."

"You really aren't going to give me an option as to whether or not to bring you into this, are you?"

"You do have an option. You can invite us to join and make it your idea, or you can deal with us following you around and doing what we would do if you had just invited us." Jason shrugged. "Same outcome, but I think one would make you feel better."

"Fine. Would you two please join me?"

"We thought you would never ask," Taylor answered with a grin. "So, now that's out of the way, I have something to show both of you tomorrow. I think you'll enjoy it."

"Can't wait," Lance replied, though rather unconvincingly.

"I'm going to go put some finishing touches on the surprise. Don't take unnecessary risks with your health, Lance. If Jason can handle it solo, let him."

"Alright, let's go! Do I get a cool baton thingy, too, or does that come when I get a promotion?" Jason asked as they left the stairwell, causing Lance to turn back to Taylor with a look of contempt as Taylor stifled a laugh.

Lance and Jason made their way toward the library at a slower pace than Lance was accustomed to going. With Lance's injuries, he hobbled alongside Jason, who, at six-foot-four, had a solid two inches on him and a longer stride than he was used to. Lance walked Jason through what a typical night of his rounds looked like and the fundamentals of using the nightstick.

"Why do I need to use your stick?" Jason asked as Lance was explaining how to hold it. "I'm much better with my hands."

"I know, and for the most part, you can use your hands. But I want people to think it's me. I don't want them thinking that anyone can just come out here and fight; the last thing this campus needs is a bunch of nuts running around trying to stop crime." Jason cocked his head to the side and looked at him. "Trust me, one nut is enough. If anything happens tonight, I want them to think it was the same person who had already been doing it."

"And the stick is what you think will make the difference? No one's going to be worried about how you grew three inches and were suddenly black?"

"Two inches. And trust me, when someone gets confronted by a maniac in a hoodie who is carrying a nightstick, they think you're six ten regardless of what your actual height is. And they don't know my skin color because I wear a hood. You will also be wearing a hood. And I doubt that if we do happen to come across someone tonight, I will have faced them before, so they won't know what the vigilante is supposed to look like. Hailey hasn't exactly gotten my bio and all of my vitals to put in the paper yet. All she knows is that I wear a hood, which means that's all that anyone knows. Now, let's head to the union. The courtyard balcony is a good spot to camp out. We can see and hear most of what happens in the heart of campus, but it's not easy to see people up there. Though I may need some help getting up the ladder."

The first night with a partner passed by in silence. Jason helped Lance back down the ladder, and the two returned home. He had to admit, it was nice being with someone throughout the night. The late-night routine was even more tiring with how beat up he was, and by the time they made it back, he didn't even take the time to change clothes or crawl under the sheets; he collapsed on top of his comforter and fell asleep immediately.

"Lance." Taylor shook Lance's shoulder. "Lance, wake up."

Lance groaned as he lifted his head off his pillow.

"Good, you're up. Come to the living room."

Taylor walked out of the room as Lance planted his face into his pillow to moan again. He reluctantly got up and stumbled into the apartment's living room to find an equally disgruntled Jason.

"What's the deal, Jansen?"

"Seriously, Taylor." Jason rubbed sleep out of his eyes. "It's a Saturday, and it's not seven a.m. yet. This is the only day I get to sleep in, so you better have a good reason for this. I understand why Lance always looks so tired now. Those late nights aren't easy."

"I told you that I had a surprise for today. I've been up for two hours trying to be patient. Clearly, I've failed. So just humor me, get dressed and let's go. We can take my car."

Fifteen minutes later, Jason and Lance had gotten dressed and ready and were in the car with Taylor. Two blocks down the road, Taylor pulled into the Castle Storage Facility across the street from the southernmost part of campus. Once he got in front of one of the larger units on the corner closest to the campus, Taylor pulled to a stop.

"You woke me up at seven a.m. on a Saturday to show me a storage unit? This had better be an entrance to Narnia, or we're going to have some serious problems," Jason threatened from the back seat.

"It may not be Narnia, but I think you will like what is on the other side of the door. I've made a few, shall we say, improvements to it. This is what I was doing all day yesterday. Come, take a look at what I've done so far." Taylor walked up to the door, unlocked it, and then backed out so that Jason and Lance could step in and flip the lights on.

"Wow" was all Jason could say.

Lance couldn't even manage that much, speechless, they wandered through what Taylor had created.

"I didn't realize they made storage units this big," Lance finally said.

"They do when you can offer to pay double on a twelve-month lease in advance. I guess some of the units have removable walls for people who want to keep boats or RVs in them. So, how would you two like a tour of the new base?" he asked, leading them to the northwest corner. "Here, on the north wall, we have a weightlifting area to work out with at any time."

Lance and Jason walked through this area, touching the different stations, moving from the bench to the squat rack and finally to the salmon ladder.

"Right next to it," Taylor continued, "we have the weapons rack." Again, Lance and Jason stopped to touch the wooden rack and pick up each weapon. "Currently, I only have a couple of wooden poles and some escrima sticks. Hopefully, we can expand this to include better weaponry in the near future so that you two can spar and take different weapons out on rounds if you need or want to. That's going to be a project for Jason to work on. Here, in the northeast corner, we have the computer setup. Four monitors and a communication station will allow me to watch all of the campus while you're on your rounds and alert you if something is happening. The next station on the east wall is the medical area. We have a bed and most of my supplies, so if you get any injuries, I can take care of them as soon as possible. Next, we have

Jason's area here in the southeast corner." When Jason saw this area, his eyes widened, and he started bouncing on his toes, thinking of the possibilities. "I've got you a table and some tools along with any parts I could find so you can work on building new technology that will help us either with communicating to Lance or to help Lance be able to protect the campus better."

Taylor continued with Lance to the middle of the building, having lost Jason to his new toys. "Finally, here in the center is a padded sparring circle for you two to train either with each other or with the dummies along the south wall. What do you think?"

"Taylor, this is incredible, but there's no way I could ask you to spend this kind of money for this. Double for twelve months? I can't accept this."

"You're kidding me, right? I've paid for both yours and Jason's rent for three years, and finally, I get to do something awesome with my dad's money, and you're turning me down? Not happening. Besides, it wasn't even that expensive. The twelve-month lease on the unit cost around five thousand dollars. The weights, weapons, and sparring areas cost about a thousand. I already had most of the computer and medical supplies, so all that stuff cost just an extra five hundred dollars. Jason's area and all the tables cost about a thousand dollars, too. That's just seventy-five hundred. I've spent that much on the two of your rent for this year alone. This isn't something you can decline or that you can return, Lance. I'm in this, too, now. We're partners."

"I don't know what to say."

"You don't need to say anything. I'm doing this because I believe in you and what you're doing. Keep protecting the campus, and we'll call it even."

"You've got yourself a deal."

"Lance!" Jason shouted from the other side. "You ready to start training?" he asked, picking up a pole from the weapons rack.

"Have you even looked at your station?" Lance asked.

"I sure have. And trust me, you will have a much larger arsenal of weapons in the near future, both for sparring and your rounds. For now, though, we have these wooden weapons. Now, come get one of your puny batons, and let's train. Here's your chance to teach me how to fight like you do."

"Not today, Jason." Taylor stepped in before Lance could accept. "Lance still has a couple more days of recovering before he can spar. You can use one of the dummies if you like, but Lance is off-limits until at least Friday."

"Fine. Then, when you come back on Friday, we're going to have some real weapons to fight with," he said, putting the pole back on the rack and heading toward his station again.

"And what can I do until Friday?"

"You can come with me to the computers so I can show you how all of this works. I'm going to install a smaller version of what I have here on each of our laptops so we can know what's happening even if we can't make it to the base."

Most of the day was spent with Taylor teaching Jason and Lance how to operate the computer systems. Taylor had gotten into the campus's security system so he would be alerted when security was, and he also used their security cameras to watch the campus on his monitors. The three finally left the base at four to eat their first meal of the day. Over the next week, they continued to learn the intricacies of the base Taylor had built. With the computers and communication now available, Lance agreed to let Jason handle the rounds solo as long as he agreed to wear an earpiece and at least carry the nightstick with him. While Lance was out with his injuries, he spent most of the time that he would have normally been on rounds discussing ideas of how to stop this new drug ring with Taylor.

TEN

It was eleven o'clock at night, and the rain was coming down hard as they sat in the base. Taylor sat silently in front of the monitor, trying to keep tabs on all the cameras, but he was having a much more difficult time than usual due to the poor visibility. Jason hadn't said a word in forty-five minutes as he worked in his corner, tools buzzing off and on as he tinkered with some new creation. Lance was propped up on the medical bed doing homework, but the constant patter of rain on the tin roof prevented him from focusing.

"This is pointless," Lance muttered, setting his book down and hopping up off the bed.

He grimaced as he reached for his side. The abrupt move aggravated his injuries. Gathering himself, he walked to the weights.

"Absolutely not." Taylor had turned from the monitor, shaking his head at Lance. "You're not healthy enough to work out yet. You are going to set yourself back even further. Jason is going to end up being the permanent vigilante if you don't learn to take care of yourself."

"No thanks," Jason responded without looking up from his work.

"Well, what do you want me to do?" Lance asked. "I can't study with that constant *ping-ping-pinging* on the roof. I don't have anything else productive to do like you and Jason do. It's miserable being sidelined like this."

"If you want, you can take a shift watching the monitors. Normally, it doesn't affect me, but trying to look for things through the rain is really straining my eyes."

"Fine. Whatever it takes to do something."

Lance walked in front of the monitor while Taylor took his place on the bed as Jason continued at his workstation. Taylor pulled out his own textbook and began reading.

Lance yawned as midnight approached. *What is even the point of all this tonight?* He asked himself. He knew he had driven home the point that the vigilante always had to be on duty, or the campus could lose trust, *but come on. It's a downpour out there. No one is going to be out doing things tonight.* He let his heavy eyes close for a beat. Then two. He opened them as wide as he could and blinked rapidly, trying to stay awake. Movement on the screen caught his eye as someone ran from the top of the screen through the bottom before another person entered the screen also running.

"Jason, you're on," Lance called from the monitor.

"What do you mean?" Jason asked, looking up.

Taylor sat his book down and looked over, too.

"I mean, you're on! There was someone who just ran through the monitor being chased by someone else. They look like they're heading toward us from the union. Grab the nightstick and an earpiece and go!"

Jason and Taylor both jumped up. Jason grabbed his hoodie while Taylor got him the earpiece. Lance tossed Jason the nightstick, and he was out the door.

Lance and Taylor huddled around the monitors. Jason appeared as a monitor switched to the camera closest to them on campus. He disappeared as he ran out of the camera's frame before reappearing in a different square. Then the monitor switched cameras again, and he was gone. In his place were two people running, with the second person having significantly cut down the distance Lance had seen at first.

"Jason," Taylor said into the earpiece, "it looks like they're heading for the street in front of you. You've got about two hundred feet before the intersection point."

Taylor tapped on the keyboard, and the four boxes of video feed transitioned into one camera angle. Five seconds after Taylor gave Jason the intersection point, the two people exited the alley between two buildings. The chaser lunged at their victim and knocked them to the ground before they made it to the road. The victim swung their fist once before their arm was pinned to the ground. The attacker pulled their fist back to swing, but then Jason entered the frame. Without slowing from his sprint, Jason left his feet and tackled the attacker, taking him off the victim.

The camera showed Jason swinging the nightstick into the attacker before punching him once. Jason sat there for a few beats, catching his breath before standing up and returning to the victim. As he crouched to check on the victim, Taylor turned from the computer and pulled out his phone.

"Hello?" Taylor asked. "Yes, I-I just saw someone being attacked on Oak Street between Fourth and Fifth. I-I think they're okay now. It looks like the vigilante saved them. I-I just wanted the police to know so they could come take care of the attacker. Thank you."

He hung up and looked up to see Lance staring at him.

"I didn't want the cops showing up too early before Jason was able to get away, but I also wanted to make sure the guy he just took out didn't get away."

"That makes sense, but what was the stammering about?"

"I wanted to sound like someone who just witnessed an attack and was shaken. Didn't want to raise any suspicion."

"Smart."

They watched as blue-and-red lights cut through the dark and rainy scene on the screen. Jason ran into the alley between buildings as the lights pulled up to find the victim standing and rubbing their neck while the attacker was still strewn out on the ground.

Taylor closed the feed, and the monitor showed four boxes once again. Lance returned to the medical bed and hopped onto it to wait for Jason. Three minutes later, the door flew open and Jason came in drenched from the rain.

"That was exhilarating!" he screamed as he peeled off his hoodie and hung it up on the squat rack to dry. "I can't believe you were holding out on me with this, Lance!"

"I mean, I had only intervened twice before you two found me unconscious, so I wasn't really holding out on much. It can be exhilarating, though," he admitted.

"What happened?" Taylor asked, walking over from the monitor.

"The guy I saved said the other one was his girlfriend's ex. He had been harassing her, and so the guy convinced his girlfriend to get a restraining order. The ex found out and tried to jump him tonight. The guy fought him off at first. Then the ex pulled a knife, and the guy ran. I don't know if you could see through the rain, but the ex was about to stab him when I got there."

"We couldn't see the knife," Taylor answered, shaking his head. "That's terrifying. He could have killed him."

"That's why the campus needs the vigilante. No matter who's under the hood." Lance answered, slapping Jason's wet shoulder.

"We really got to keep some towels around here," Jason said, pulling his wet shirt away from his skin where Lance had hit. "And maybe a change of clothes, too."

"Ha," Taylor laughed. "Let's go ahead and call it a night and head to the apartment. I'll keep my laptop with me in case something happens, but Jason deserves some dry clothes, and I think we've all had enough of being in here in the rain for one night."

"Agreed," Lance and Jason answered together.

They shut down the base and ran to Taylor's car in the rain.

VIGILANTE SHINES BRIGHT ON RAINY NIGHT

It was a dark and stormy night last night as Jake Bridges was walking to his car after a night of studying. The night got worse as Paul Lacks confronted him, brandishing a knife. Bridges had recently convinced his girlfriend to file a restraining order on Lacks, her ex, after prolonged harassment. It was this action that motivated Lacks to confront Bridges. "He chased me for almost five minutes with both of us running hard in the rain last night." Bridges told the Gazette last night. "I had almost made it to the road when he caught me and took me to the ground. I got one punch in before he pinned my arm. He pulled back his knife to stab me, and I closed my eyes. Next thing I knew, the weight was off me and Paul was yelling. I looked over and just saw the outline of a man on top of him before he went quiet. The man came and checked on me and left as the cops arrived. If it weren't for him, I'd probably be dead." The officers on the scene had no comment as to who the man who stopped this attack was, but Bridges believes it was the vigilante. "Oh, absolutely," he said. "I saw the stick. It was him. I owe him my life." This campus needs the vigilante. Tonight, he saved Jake's life. Next time, it could be yours, it could be mine. Thanking this hero again for the campus.

Hailey Hall

"On the front page with a story written by my girl-friend. Nothing can stop me today," Jason declared, walking into the base.

It was Saturday morning, and Taylor was giving Lance a physical to see if he was ready to return to the field. His bruises had all healed mostly, and he was walking miraculously well after the beating he had endured.

"You earned it, man," Lance said with a smile.

"It's weird that the one night you go out as the vigilante ends up being the longest article Hailey writes about it," Taylor observed. "You don't think she's onto us, do you?"

"No way. She'd have let me hear about it by now. I think it was just a coincidence," Jason answered as Taylor made a note on his clipboard.

"So, what's the verdict, doc?" Lance asked as Taylor laid the clipboard down.

"You're good to go. I'd say have some restraint and probably take Jason anytime you go out to be safe, but I think you're ready to get back out there."

"Finally," Lance sighed.

"Does that mean we can finally spar?" Jason asked.

"Absolutely. Just don't hurt each other."

"No promises," Jason laughed, walking to the weapons rack. He grabbed a pole and tossed Lance a wooden nightstick.

"About time," Lance said, catching the nightstick from Jason.

Taylor returned to the monitor as Lance and Jason got in fighting position. They spent the afternoon fighting before leaving to get dinner. Lance and Taylor returned to the base afterward, while Jason and Hailey had a date. They had spent more time in the base over the last week than they had in their apartment and had no intention of slowing down. Not with a campus to protect.

ELEVEN

"I hate to break up your fight, but I think you need to come take a look at this."

Lance and Jason laid their weapons down on the mat and picked up a towel, drying their sweat as they walked to Taylor's computer station to see an alert going off on a monitor.

"What's this about?" Lance asked.

"Someone else has hacked into the security system, and it appears that they've shut off all of the security for the IT store and the experimental lab behind it."

"Can't you just turn it back on?"

Taylor shook his head. "I'm just using the system. I can't control it. I could probably override it if I had a couple of hours, but we don't have that much time. There's a reason the system went down. You two will need to go over there and check things out. You think you're ready to get back out there, Lance?"

"It's about time."

Lance and Jason put on their hoodies and grabbed their weapons: the nightstick for Lance and a wooden pole for Jason. Taylor handed each of them an improved earpiece with a microphone that Jason had designed days earlier, and they crossed the street to campus.

The IT store was in Baker Hall, the building in the southeast corner of the campus quad. It took them five minutes to get to the building from the storage facility, and they arrived just as ten men came out carrying three bags. Before Lance had time to say anything, Jason had rushed the group, and Lance had little choice but to follow him. Jason made it to the group before they could hear or see him, and he dispatched two of the ten before any of them had time to react. Lance arrived and quickly took another member of the group out. The four remaining members of the group without the bags turned to face Jason and Lance as the carriers fled. Lance took one out with a couple of swings of his nightstick to the head and gave chase, leaving Jason to handle the other three.

Lance stayed in the shadows of the tree-lined sidewalk as he followed the carriers, still going at a brisk pace. While he was confident they couldn't see him, they still ran as if they knew they were being pursued. They made a couple of misdirection turns and after evasive running, they seemed to decide they were just being paranoid and continued on their way at a much more manageable pace, allowing Lance to mercifully transition from running to a jog.

The carriers crossed the street and entered the neighborhood that was home to the Greek houses. Lance had a more challenging time staying in the shadows as they left the trees, but he had avoided being spotted to this point. They stopped at the fence of the Kappa Beta Kappa house, where they tossed their bags over the fence before climbing it themselves. Lance jogged up to the fence after they had all made it over and peaked over the fence line to see where they went next.

There was a large shed in the yard where twenty to thirty people appeared to be waiting for the carriers. Knowing he couldn't take on thirty people and fearing he would be found if he stayed much longer, Lance took what he knew back to the base. He carefully walked back to campus and hurried back to the storage unit once he was in the familiar shadows of the campus.

"Are you kidding me?" Jason hopped off of his table as Lance walked into the unit. "How could you just leave me to fight the four who stayed? You saw a four-on-one situation and assumed I would handle it so you could run off and play detective?"

"No. What I saw was you running after them without thinking what could happen. You're the only reason there was even a fight to begin with. I wanted to know where they were trying to take all of that stuff so that we would know who we were dealing with. And I didn't leave you in a four-on-one. I took out one of the guys on my way to follow the carriers. You're welcome. Look, if you want to help me, fine, but we're not going to do this in whatever way you feel like that day. You can't just rush a group when we're outnumbered ten to two and then get mad at me for going after the people we had gone to stop."

"You two can figure this out in your next sparring session. Right now, I need each of you to tell me what happened after you split. Jason, I could keep up with you thanks to the cameras. Were you able to get any answers from the men you fought before their reinforcements showed up?"

"No, they weren't really in the talking mood."

"Lance, were you able to find anything?"

"I found where they are working out of. They have a shed in the backyard of the Kappa Beta Kappa house. Around thirty guys were waiting for the carriers when they got back. I left after that. I saw a lot more potential for something bad happening at that point than something good."

"Were you able to figure out what it was they stole?"

"I was not."

"Jason?"

"Again, they weren't really talkative."

Taylor paced between the two tables, thinking. Jason and Lance sat silently with their heads down as if they were in trouble. After almost a minute of pacing, Taylor finally stopped and talked to them again.

"OK, I'll start working on tracking down the hacker. If we can find whoever it was that shut down the security system, they should be able to lead us to the top. You two keep training."

And with that, Taylor turned his back to them and typed away. He had brought a new chair into the unit, switching out the one in the base for his chair in the apartment because of the time he had been spending at the base, which only increased the time he was spending there. He was constantly checking his monitors, even in the daytime, making sure he missed nothing. Jason and Lance were starting to worry about how often he was working there and reminded him that the cameras were on his laptop, too, but to no avail.

Jason and Lance weren't dying to spar with one another, afraid the other would be looking to make a point after their argument earlier, so they sat on the bench next to the weights and tried to figure out if this theft was connected to the drug ring they had uncovered.

"Why would they need something from the IT store to make drugs?" Jason asked. "And it seems they already had most of the tools needed since they had already made a batch for the guy they're working for. What we know isn't adding up."

"Maybe this thing is more than just drugs. We don't really know much right now. The drugs could just be the tip of the iceberg. We can't even be positive that these are the same two groups."

"If these drugs can do what you say they can, that's a pretty big tip."

"That's what I'm afraid of," Lance answered. "Especially now that I know he has an entire fraternity under his control. I thought it was just a small group, but after seeing a shed full of guys in the fraternity's backyard, I have to believe it's the whole organization."

"Which fraternity did you say it was?"

"Kappa Beta Kappa."

"I'll look into them and see if I can find anything that could help us. I have some friends on the interfraternity council. Maybe they can help us out. Could you see if this 'professor' was there tonight?"

Lance shook his head. "No, I just saw it was a big crowd. When you check with your contacts, see if you can find anything about professors this frat is connected to."

"Lance!" Taylor called from the computer. "While Jason does that, you may want to go back out. I just saw a couple of guys following some girls to the library. Once the girls went in, they ducked into the shadows near the picnic tables. You might want to check this out."

"I agree. I'll head that way." Lance grabbed his hoodie from the bench and his nightstick from the weapons rack. He checked to ensure he still had the earpiece in this hoodie, putting it on as he headed for the library.

Lance crossed the street and made his way to the library. He slowed down as he walked past Baker Hall to ensure the group hadn't left anything earlier. They hadn't. He continued to the library, making it in ten minutes after leaving the base. His training seemed to be paying off; he had been making it around campus much quicker than when he had first started, even while still sore. He walked behind the building so they wouldn't see him coming, but when he came around the other side, they weren't where Taylor had said they had hidden.

"Taylor, where did they go?"

"They left right before you arrived. The girls left while you were behind the library. Just follow the sidewalk toward the dorms. You should be able to catch them, but hurry."

Lance broke into a jog down the sidewalk. He saw two groups of people not far ahead of him. As he got closer, both groups walked faster, and the men tried to push the girls into the space between two buildings. Lance broke into a sprint. As he approached, one of the men pulled his arm back as the girls put their arms up to protect their heads, one stepping in front of the other. Instead of feeling a strike, though, they heard a man screaming as if he had been shot. Lowering their arms and looking up, they found he may have been better off having been shot. His arm dangled loosely from his elbow down, blowing in the wind like a branch hanging on to a tree by a few threads.

The man Lance had hit fell to his knees, clutching at his arm while the other tried to flee. Lance gave chase but struggled to catch up. The man risked a look back as he neared the end of the building, only to see Lance's nightstick hurtling toward him. The man dropped to the ground as the nightstick crashed into the brick, missing him by a hair. Before he could get back to his feet, though, Lance had covered the distance between them and put him back on the ground with one hit to the back of the head. Lance hit him twice more, and the man slumped over, unconscious. Lance walked to where his nightstick had fallen to find it lying in the alley in two pieces.

He picked up the pieces and put them in his hoodie. He dragged the man back to the sidewalk and dropped him next to the one whose arm he had dislocated, who was now also clutching his groin and struggling to breathe. Lance looked up from the man at the two girls.

"He tried to run away," the one who had stepped in front of her friend answered with a shrug.

She was around Hailey's height and was wearing a Franklin Soccer T-shirt. Her blonde hair was pulled into a ponytail, and even in this darkness, Lance could see some of the bluest eyes he had ever seen. Her friend was slightly shorter with green eyes and had her curly red hair in a bun on the top of her head.

"Are you two okay?" he growled at them.

"Yes," the blonde answered again. "They had just really caught up to us when you showed up."

Lance looked away and turned his mic back on. To Taylor, he said, "Can you alert the police?"

"They're on the way. I contacted them as soon as you brought the second guy out from the alley. They should arrive within the minute."

Lance looked back to the girls.

"The police will be here shortly. Is there anything else I can do for you before I leave? I prefer to avoid the police."

"Can you knock him out like you did the other guy?"

Lance looked down at the man still clutched over with his one good arm, who looked up with a yell as Lance's fist came down twice, knocking him unconscious as well.

"Anything else?"

"I think we're good. Thank you again. Um, I didn't catch your name," she said with a smile.

"Nice try," Lance laughed. "If you think of something clever between now and when Hailey Hall shows up asking questions—and believe me, she will—feel free to give me a good name. I'm starting to get tired of being called the vigilante. It doesn't have that nice of a ring to it, and I think it's hurting my branding."

Sirens grew louder. The girls both looked toward the road the sirens were coming from and when they looked back, Lance had disappeared into the shadows.

"Very smooth, Locke," Jason greeted with a grin as Lance walked back into the unit.

"Thanks, Morgan. But on to more pressing matters, I need you to put that station of yours to good use. I may have gotten a scratch on the nightstick tonight." He pulled the two pieces out and laid them on the table.

Jason whistled as he looked at it. "I can put it back together, but it will only be good for show. You know, like how your dad meant for it to be used when he gave it to you. Don't worry, though," he continued, "I've been working on some new weapons, and I should have them finished soon. Until then, you can use the sparring weapons. I really can't wait to read Hailey's piece in the morning. I hope that girl gave you some ridiculous name. I bet she called you her fairy godmother."

chapter

TWELVE

WHITE KNIGHT RIDES AGAIN

The campus vigilante was in action again last night, and this time with a new name. At one-thirty this morning, freshmen Ashley Adair and Nicole Kirk were leaving the library after printing out their government papers. On their way back to their dorm room, they heard footsteps behind them as two men appeared on the sidewalk after they had thought they were alone. They sped up, but that only caused the men to move faster as well. The men caught up to them between Carpenter Hall and Mulder Hall and tried to maneuver them into the shadows between the two buildings. As one man, Hector Jackson, drew back his arm to strike Ashley, the girls heard a scream. They looked up to see the attacker curled over, clutching at his limp forearm that had been dislocated. The second man attempted to flee, and the vigilante gave chase. Less than a minute later, he returned, dragging the man, Larry Price, back to the sidewalk unconscious. As the vigilante returned, he called in the police and turned to leave, but not before checking on the victims. 'He made sure to check on us and make sure that we didn't need an ambulance or anything like that.' Adair told me, 'I tried to get his name, but he wasn't exactly forthcoming. Though he did suggest Nicole and I come up with a new moniker for him because he wasn't very fond of being called the vigilante. We tried to think of something clever, but the best we could come up with was the Knight. He came in like a white knight to help us when we most needed it. Actually, that might be better. The White Knight. That sounds more like a hero's name.' And a hero this White Knight is. Once again, on behalf of the student body, we say thank you to the White Knight.

Hailey Hall

"The White Knight. I like it."

Lance sat Hailey's article, which Jason had brought back to the apartment after his class that morning, on the armrest of the couch.

"Good to hear. That means you'll love what I've been working on."

"What have you been working on?"

"Soon. Very soon."

"What does that even mean?" Lance asked, but Jason wasn't saying anything more on the subject. "Taylor, you know what he's working on?"

"No idea. Nice article in the paper, though. We need to get you an interview or something with Hailey. 'White Knight tells all.' That would be great for your PR."

Lance stood, shaking his head. "Not a chance," he laughed. He grabbed his bag and headed out the door.

He was headed to meet Hailey, but just as Lance. He had no desire for anyone other than Jason and Taylor to know his secret. He hadn't exactly wanted them to know either, but that was out of his control. What he did need, though, was help with his Spanish. And since Gwen still wasn't talking to him, Hailey was his next best option.

He got to the union at eleven-ten. The ten-thirty classes hadn't let out yet, so the food court was empty. He bought a chicken sandwich and looked for an empty booth to wait for Hailey. He found one tucked in the corner, picked up his own copy of the paper, and looked over Hailey's article again as he ate his sandwich. He didn't get either of the girls' names, so he couldn't be sure, but he assumed Ashley was the blonde who had done all the talking last night. The red-haired girl didn't say a word to him last night, and he doubted Hailey had gotten much from her either.

"Pretty great journalism you've got there, wouldn't you say, Locke?"

"It's not too shabby, Hall," Lance conceded with a smile, looking up from the paper to see Hailey sitting across from him. He hadn't even realized she had shown up. "It's good to see our hero finally has a name. Those girls didn't do too bad coming up with it, either. Looks like you missed your chance to name a hero, Hall. Can't believe you didn't try to beat them to the punch. How many chances will you actually get to name a superhero?"

"I thought about that, too. I should have come up with a name for him sooner. Although I have to say, their name is pretty spot on for our man, don't you think? Maybe he'll do some things to incorporate the name and make it stick."

"Like start riding a horse or wearing a suit of armor? Somehow, I doubt that."

"I guess you're right." Hailey laughed. "Did you bring your Spanish homework?"

"Yes. I was able to get most of it done. I just had a couple of problems that I wasn't sure what to do."

"Would one of those problems be talking to Gwen?"

"Excuse me?"

Hailey rolled her eyes. "Come on, Locke. I know you two are fighting, even if she won't say it. I would talk to her about it, but considering it happened the day after our little chat with Jason and Taylor, I have a pretty good idea what you fought about, and I'd rather not approach that with her again unless I have to. What's going on?"

"Basically, what you're assuming happened. I tried to tell her I was stressed about the fact that I have no clue what I'll be doing in three months, but she didn't buy it. She said that she knew I was upset about what happened to her, and then she got upset and told me she would see me at Taylor's birthday. I've tried calling her, but she's still pretty upset. Taylor's birthday is this weekend, so I'm hoping she will have cooled off enough to talk by then."

"And are you still upset about what happened to her?"

"Honestly? Yeah. I am. I know it's stupid, but I still feel responsible. I mean, how can I not?"

"I'm still upset. I know Jason and Taylor are, too. I'd be shocked if you weren't still upset. But you know how you have processed that has just been putting more weight on Gwen, right?"

"I didn't before, but I see it now. I had been so focused on my own guilt that I hadn't realized how it was affecting Gwen. Jason and Taylor called me out on it after all of you had talked about it. I got pretty upset when they brought it up, but they were right. I had just internalized it so much and tried to hide it that I had lost sight of what was happening. I think this is the first time I've actually admitted any of this out loud. I miss us hanging out. All of us together, but also just me and her. I don't know what to do."

"Tell her what you just told me. Tell her how it affect-ed you and that you're still upset about what happened but that you're working through it. You know how much she hates it when people try to protect her. Just tell her how you feel. All of how you feel."

"I don't know what you mean."

"Yes, you do."

"Okay. Are you going to help me with my Spanish or not? This is due in a couple hours, and I have half of the questions completely blank."

Hailey let the conversation return to his homework and didn't push Lance to talk about his feelings for Gwen anymore. They finished thirty minutes before his class and headed over to Gibson Hall together, where they had separate Spanish classes. Lance found a desk near the back and settled in but could keep hearing Hailey's voice in his head even as his professor walked in and greeted the class. *Just tell her how you feel. All of how you feel.*

"Taylor, how long have you been here?" Jason asked as he and Lance walked into the base.

Taylor had been at the computer station when Jason and Lance had left last night, and they found him in the same spot now. His obsessiveness with the monitors was worrying.

"I've only been here for about an hour and a half. I think I'm getting close to finding the hacker."

"Get some rest, man. We would be better off waiting to find the hacker and having you at full speed."

"Fine. You're right. I just really want to figure this out. They're good. What are you two going to do?"

"We're going to lift some, then Jason is going to work on some weapons, and I'm going back to the room to get some sleep myself."

"I'll wake both of you up when I get back to the room, and we can get some dinner. Now, go get some rest, Taylor. Don't make Lance put you to sleep when he gets home."

Taylor left as Jason and Lance made their way over to the lifting area. They stretched, then transitioned to the bench. They each did three sets before moving on from there to the squat rack and then finishing on the salmon ladder. They finished by stretching again. Jason walked to his table and finished up his repair job on the nightstick while Lance did a scan of the monitors to make sure nothing out of the ordinary was going on. Lance began to leave, but Jason stopped him to show him the repaired nightstick.

"It's as good as new. From an aesthetic perspective, that is. From a functional one, it's useless. It would shatter immediately. But a keepsake nonetheless."

"At least now it's a keepsake with fond memories. Thanks, Jason. I really do appreciate you fixing it, even if I can't use it anymore. How's it going with the new weapon?"

"Almost there. I'm just having to put some finishing touches on it."

"Have you been working on a weapon for when you go out as well?"

"I have some ideas for that, as well as extra weapons, just in case we have more specific needs, but I'm taking care of yours first."

Lance left for the apartment with the nightstick in his box while Jason turned back to his desk. He reached underneath the bench and pulled out a box of his own. After taking the weapon out and placing it on the table in front of him, he began his work.

He started with the handle, putting a black leather wrap around it to make it more comfortable for Lance as he was fighting. The cushion should help keep his hand from tiring if he ever had to fight for longer than a couple of minutes. The only part of the handle not covered in leather was a button that would attach to the wire he needed to place next. He pulled the wire from his toolbox and hooked it up to the button first. He then gently threaded it into the groove down the middle of the weapon. He flipped it over and did the same to this side.

After the wires were in place, he sealed them in to ensure they would stay in contact with the metal body of the weapon even while Lance was using it. He pressed the button, lowered the weapon against the metal table before him, and smiled as sparks jumped from the point of contact. He took his finger off the button and returned to work on the weapon. He rounded the sides down to where they were blunt enough that Lance wouldn't have to be worried about killing someone when he was swinging it.

Jason stood from his desk, looked at the weapon in his outstretched arm, and admired his work. He made his way behind his table and took the sheet off of a glass case and a stand to put the case on. He walked both to the center of the room and set them up. Inside the case, he placed the weapon on a small rack to display it. He looked at the handle at the top, perfectly wrapped with black strips of leather with a shiny white knob at the end. He continued down to the cross-section where the handle met the body, where the cross-section curved downward to provide a measure of protection for the hands while fighting; this, too, was a bright white. He continued to the gleaming steel body with the barely discernible source of electricity that could short-circuit the room he was standing in and could also inflict varying levels of pain on a person, if necessary. Then he made it to where the two sides came to a point at the end of the sword.

Jason gazed at the tip, which, unlike the sides that Jason had dulled, was sharp enough to draw blood just by touching it. He hoped Lance would not need to use this function of the sword, but he didn't want him to need to pierce something and be left with a dull blade. He took one last look at it before covering the case and turning off the lights, still grinning over his work.

THIRTEEN

Jason, Lance, and Taylor went straight from dinner to their base, walking the short distance from the campus cafeteria to the storage unit in under ten minutes. Jason stepped back as Taylor and Lance walked into the room in front of him. They stopped right inside the doorway as they turned on the light. They both looked back at Jason after seeing the sheet-covered display case in the center of the room.

"What's this?" Lance asked.

Jason smiled but didn't answer. Instead, he walked to the case and pulled the sheet off, revealing the sword underneath.

"Is this . . ."

Lance couldn't convince himself that what he was looking at was what he thought it was.

"Your new weapon? Yes, it is. With your preference for a smaller weapon like the nightstick, I doubted you would want some sort of pole like I've been using. I also remember you saying your dad had you take fencing classes when you were younger. This seemed like a pretty good weapon for you. And," his grin got even wider, "after they named you the White Knight, it appears I made a good decision."

"Don't you think this weapon is too dangerous for Lance to use?" Taylor finally found his voice. "He's not exactly in the business of decapitating people. He just knocks them out and leaves them for the police."

Jason reached into the case and pulled out the sword. Holding it in his right hand, he stretched out his left arm. He opened his left hand and quickly struck it with the sword. Lance and Taylor both jumped toward him, but they were too late.

"Ha!" Jason laughed and opened his left hand to reveal that there wasn't a scratch. "I rounded out both sides," he said, opening and closing his hand for them to see. "It's still a very hard surface, but you're not going to slice through someone. I did leave the tip sharpened, though. If you do need to pierce something or someone, you'll be able to; you'll just have to use the point for that."

He handed the sword over to Lance. Lance took it and tossed the sword from hand to hand to check the weight and to judge how it sat in his hands. He had always loved swords. Fencing was the only class his dad made him take that he had actually enjoyed. He moved the sword slowly through the air, going through moves ingrained in his mind he had learned years ago, his hands grasping the leather-wrapped hilt. The sword was much bigger than the foil, but he was also stronger now, and the moves were still useful, even if it was a larger weapon. The nightstick felt like a tool in his hand, but this . . . this felt like an extension of his arm.

"What does this button on the handle do?" he asked as his hand brushed against the button Jason had placed on the hilt.

"That," Jason said as he grabbed a piece of paper from his desk, "creates a wave of electricity throughout the body of the sword. Press it."

Lance did, and the sword crackled as it was suddenly charged. Jason crumpled up the paper into a ball and tossed it toward the sword. When Lance made contact with the ball, it blackened and then caught on fire as it fell to the ground where it burned itself up. Jason walked to the door and hit the light switch, thrusting them into darkness.

"Hit it again," Jason instructed.

Lance did so, and the sword crackled once again, this time lighting up. A bluish-white light illuminated Lance and a small area around him as the electricity coursed through the sword. Jason turned the lights back on and walked to where Lance and Taylor were standing.

"So, what do you think?"

"I love it."

"I had hoped you would. Taylor and I have a couple more surprises we're working on, but we haven't quite finished those up yet. Go ahead and practice your swordsmanship on the dummies."

"Just don't stab them," Taylor added.

Lance walked to the dummies as Jason and Taylor walked to each of their stations. Jason was deep at work on some new communication tech while Taylor was trying to find the hacker again. Lance slowly went through moves he had learned when he was younger to get more acquainted with his sword. Every fencing move might not be fit for a sword like this, but some could still prove useful.

"We got him!"

Two hours had passed when Taylor yelled out his triumphant scream. Lance and Jason stopped what they were doing and rushed over to the computer to see what Taylor was talking about.

"He hacked into the security system again while I was looking for him. We have him. His IP, his location, everything we need. Lance, he just shut off the security in Gibson. They must need more of the chemicals to make their drugs. You need to get over there now. We can take care of the hacker later now that we have all this."

Lance put his hoodie on, grabbed his sword, and was almost to the door when Jason shouted at him.

"You forgot this," he said as he handed Lance a belt and sheath. "You would look pretty weird just walking around holding a sword. The sheath might be a weird look, too, but it's at least a little less noticeable than someone running around holding on to a sword."

"Good call." Lance thanked him and put the sword into the sheath. He crossed the street to campus and was almost to Gibson when Taylor's voice came into his earpiece.

"He just left. He's headed toward the Kappa house by himself. Make sure you get the chemicals from him and get him, too, if you can."

Lance sprinted to cut the thief off before the house. Taylor kept him updated as to where the thief was. And if Lance could make it to the road separating the Greek houses from campus, he could cut off the thief, who had taken a path with more shadows. As Lance neared the road, he also saw the thief approaching the street. Lance broke into a full-on sprint, catching the thief by the shoulder as he stepped into the road. Lance grabbed the bag from the thief's arm and backed away from him. Lance was still out of breath from the chase and was hoping the thief would follow him for a little bit as he caught his breath.

The thief followed but gave Lance little time to catch his breath as he rushed him as soon as Lance stopped moving. As the thief approached, Lance drew his sword and made sure that his hand was on the button, causing the sword to glow as it left the sheath. Lance stepped into a stance, holding the illuminated sword in front of him as the thief stumbled at the sight of the weapon. The thief paused only for a second, but it was all the hesitation Lance needed. He swung the body of the sword, no longer lit up, into the legs of the thief, eliciting a yelp as the thief fell to the ground. The man got a kick into Lance's stomach that knocked the little breath he had left out of him. Lance responded to that by thrusting the sword's hilt into the thief's temple three times in succession, knocking him out.

Lance returned the sword to its sheath and spoke into the headset. "I'm bringing him back in so we can have a chat."

Lance bent down, lifted the man by his underarms, and dragged him back toward the base. The man was Lance's height and probably a little heavier. Even in as good of shape as he had gotten in the last month, he was still pushing himself, even dragging this guy back to the base.

"Lance,"—Taylor's voice cut through the earpiece—"you've got company." Lance dragged the body off the sidewalk and into the alleyway as students passed. "Hold tight," Taylor said as the group passed in front of him. "It looks like there was something happening in Mulder tonight. A bunch of students are all trickling out now."

"Great," Lance muttered, dropping the thief to the ground.

Ten minutes passed before Taylor's voice was back in his ear.

"It looks like . . . of students . . . problem . . ."

"You're cutting out, man. What did you say?"

". . . hear me? . . . . Lance? . . . Hurry . . . Get there . . ."

Lance pulled the box the earpiece was connected to out of his hoodie pocket. It was bent from the kick he took. Shaking his head and shoving it back into his pocket, he peeked out of the alley and saw it was clear. He went back and grabbed the man again and dragged him back onto the sidewalk. Lance was making slow but consistent progress back to the unit and was almost to the street that separated campus from the storage complex, when he heard a shout from the direction he had been coming from. He had been walking backward, pulling the man, but he had been looking over his shoulder for the last minute and had missed fifteen guys walking up from the Greek neighborhood.

Lance's pulse raced as he pulled the guy as quickly as he could while the group ran toward him. Lance got to the road, but there wasn't time to get across the street and to the base without leading them right to it. They were closing in on him quickly, only fifteen seconds away now.

Lance was staring at the group when tires squealed behind him.

"Get in!" Jason hopped out of the passenger side and helped Lance throw the unconscious thief into the back seat.

Lance followed into the back while Jason crawled into the front with Taylor. The car peeled out as the first of the group made it to the road and tried to hop onto it, but they fell off onto the street as Taylor accelerated.

"What was all that about?" Lance gasped as his head fell back into the headrest.

"A group from Kappa came onto the cameras right as the group from Mulder cleared. It looked like they were looking for our man back there. I tried warning you, but we couldn't get through. So, we got in my car to come get you," Taylor told him as he sped away from the storage unit, his eyes on the rearview mirror to watch the following fraternity members chasing them falling further behind.

"He got a kick in before I knocked him out. Knocked the breath out of me and bent this up. I'm thinking that was the issue with the transmission." Lance pulled out the box and earpiece and tossed it onto the center console.

"Yeah, that would do it," Jason answered, shaking his head. "I'll try and make a new one that won't have to be connected like this."

"Great." Lance rested his head again.

After a mile, Taylor took a left and circled back to the unit. Jason and Lance pulled the still unconscious thief from the back seat as they pulled to a stop next to the door. Lance stumbled over to Taylor's station, where he collapsed onto the bed. Taylor walked to where Jason was tying the thief to a chair.

"I'm going to let Lance rest until this guy starts to stir. Any idea as to how we interrogate him without giving away where and who we are?"

"I think we should shut the lights off and just put a lamp on him. Then, I would just have Lance interrogate him using his vigilante voice. Mainly because I think he sounds absolutely ridiculous using that voice. It's not like Lance is friends with half of the campus. Maybe fifteen people would recognize his voice if he were talking to them as the vigilante. And they would know who he was regardless of the voice he was using. It's absurd."

"I agree that it doesn't make much sense, but I guess it makes him feel more comfortable."

"Whatever. I still think he sounds ridiculous. Help me move this guy against the wall. We'll blindfold him for now, so we don't have to keep working with the lights off until he comes to."

Taylor obliged, and they moved the thief next to the dummies on the wall. After they finished blindfolding him and tying him up, they went to their separate stations. Taylor worked on pinpointing where they could find the hacker. A few minutes later, he had the building the computer had been in. After finishing that, he aimed to figure out what was stolen from the chemistry building. While Taylor worked on that, Jason was busy making new toys for Lance. He had needed new materials for this project, so he had to let Taylor in to get the money he needed. He hadn't realized how much some of this metal would cost. He was melting down aluminum to create a material to put around metal spheres to make them stronger. The project would solve the earpiece problem, so they just had to make it through the next couple of days without any more issues. While he waited for aluminum to melt, he went back to working on his own weapon, a wooden spear.

Jason liked the feel of wood in his hands, a trait he inherited from his father, who always preferred to build the family's furniture needs over buying them. This came just as much from his love of creating things with his hands as it did the family's strapped finances. Being the youngest of the five, Jason's father had almost accepted that none of his sons would have the same love for creating that he did.

All four of his brothers were as intelligent and athletic as Jason was; each of them played college sports at good universities, with two playing football, one basketball, and the other track, but none had the same creativity as their father or enjoyed making things with their hands the way he did. They had different intellectual interests. His oldest, Jaylen, was already a junior partner at a prestigious firm in Calvin, New York, after being a three-year starter in football for Rogers University in Pennsylvania, where he stayed for law school after getting his undergrad. The next oldest, Jefferson, had played basketball up the road in Duncan. He moved back to their hometown of Harrison, Wisconsin, to work as an accountant. Jaaron, the middle child, was also still in Harrison. He had stayed home for college, running track at Wisconsin Tech in Harrison before going to dental school at Harrison State. Jackson played football like Jaylen, but instead of choosing a prestigious academic school with a decent football program like Rogers, Jackson went to the football powerhouse of Finley University in Indiana. He was waiting to hear back about where he would go for his residency as he finished medical school at Finley.

Jason, though, showed a desire to make things from an early age. While he didn't exclusively use wood like his father, he loved the classic look and feel that wood gave and the flexibility it would give while remaining sturdy. He had spent countless hours in the shop with his dad from the time he had turned twelve, experimenting with ideas. While he was a talented athlete, he didn't have the same drive as his brothers, preferring to tinker in his father's shed over putting in extra reps. He could have played football at a lesser school, but Franklin University had offered him a full scholarship for his academics, and they had one of the top engineering programs in the nation. He had known no one else at the school at the time, but it was too good of an offer for him to pass on. And going somewhere he knew no one was also a relief. He wouldn't have to walk around with the weight of living up to his brothers' impressive accomplishments. He would have the freedom to just be Jason Morgan and be judged on that alone.

Jason had finished working on the pole of his weapon and had inserted a button and rubber-lined wire of his own through the center of the pole. He was now working on the end of his spear. He had two points on the end of his weapon. The dual points allowed him to make it less dangerous as a killing weapon while maintaining its ability to inflict pain during his fights. It was also made with Lance's sword in mind. The two points would work the same way as the charger he had created for the weapons. Jason could charge Lance's sword with his spear if he needed to while they were out on campus or wherever else they might end up.

As he finished attaching the points, the thief moaned from behind him. He got up and walked to Taylor's station, tapping Taylor on the shoulder and pointing at the thief. Taylor nodded and walked to get Lance up. Jason placed his spear on the weapons rack and walked to shut the lights off.

Taylor shook Lance's arm. "He's up."

"Got it." Lance groaned and sat up.

Taylor briefed Lance on the plan as Jason set up a lamp next to the thief.

All three walked to where the thief was sitting. Lance prepared what he would say in his head. Taylor set up a recorder so they would have what he said in case they needed to use it later, and Jason removed the blindfold once the other two were ready.

Jason and Taylor walked away as Lance prepared to question the thief. Jason had given Lance his spear and told him the voltage on his weapon was much lower. It would hurt, but it wouldn't kill him or anything if the thief wasn't being forthcoming.

Lance paced right behind the lamp they had set up. He lowered his voice and questioned the thief.

"Who is the fraternity working for?"

The thief just looked up at him with a blank look as he remained silent.

"Who are you working for?" Lance repeated.

Again, the thief said nothing, just continued to stare at the spot where Lance's voice had come from, searching for something to lock his eyes onto. Lance took the spear, rested the point against the thief's leg, and asked again.

"Who are you working for?"

The thief clenched his jaw, but stayed silent. Lance pressed the button on the spear's shaft and watched the tip light up as the smell of burnt hair and skin filled the small room as the thief let out a yelp. Lance paced again while waiting for the thief to catch his breath. Once it appeared the thief had settled down, Lance growled again, louder, and more forcefully this time.

"Who do you work for?"

"I don't know." The thief panted.

"Are you a member of the Kappa Beta Kappa fraternity?"

"Yes."

"And you know that the fraternity has been hired to create drugs for someone?"

"Yes."

"And do you know who this person is?"

"No."

"Who knows the identity of the man you work for?"

"Only the president and the small group he takes to make the deals. I'm just a sophomore. They just use me for errands like this."

Lance had an idea after he said that.

"Errands like what? What exactly were you doing?"

"You know what I was doing. I broke into Gibson Hall to steal some chemicals from the lab."

"What about the hacking of the campus's security system? Does the frat have someone in charge of the hacking?"

"We don't handle the hacking. The man we work for takes care of that."

Lance walked to where Jason and Taylor were sitting.

"Is that true, Taylor? Was the hacker not in the fraternity?" he whispered.

"No," Taylor answered. "At least the computer isn't in the fraternity. It was an address from the other side of campus."

Lance nodded and then walked back over to where the thief was sitting.

"What can you tell me about the professor?"

"Not much. Again, they don't let underclassmen in on those things. I know they're working with a researcher, but that's all I know, I swear."

"I believe you."

Lance turned off the lamp and then struck the thief, knocking him unconscious once more. He walked to the door and turned the lights back on.

"Taylor, I need you to download that recording onto a flash drive. All I need is the part where he admits to breaking into the lab and stealing the chemicals. Jason, I need you to help me get him to the police station. We're going to tie him up outside and leave a note, the chemicals, and the recording in his pocket." Taylor walked to him with the file already in his hand. "Taylor, I also need you to type up the note for the police and another one for Hailey. Tell the police that we caught him breaking into the lab and are just returning him to where he belongs. Sign it, the White Knight. On the note to Hailey, just tell her to check the police station. Sign that one, too. We'll leave it on her porch after we drop him off at the station."

chapter

FOURTEEN

SLEEPLESS KNIGHT

The White Knight was at work once again last night; this time, he was catching a thief who had broken into the chemistry lab in Gibson Hall. At three-thirty this morning, I received notice that there was an arrest that involved the White Knight. Upon my arrival at the station, I found officers standing around a man tied to a pole right outside the station. In the man's pockets were stolen chemicals, a recorded confession, and a note signed by the White Knight detailing what the thief had done. While I could not view the note, the officer who pulled the contents out of the thief's pocket informed me that this was what the note said. If any more information is made available, I will post it in tomorrow's edition of the Franklin Gazette, but it seems to be a straightforward incident. Once again, we say thank you to the White Knight for watching over our campus.

Hailey Hall

Lance and Jason stood behind Taylor at the computer the next night as Taylor showed them where the hacker had been working from.

"This isn't a house; it's a closed-down warehouse," Taylor told them. "I couldn't figure out who's been paying for the warehouse, but I'm guessing it's whoever is funding the fraternity as well. I doubt anyone will be there now, but I still think you should check out the building. Jason made some motion sensors that will trigger this camera." He handed them a compact camera. "You'll put this in the warehouse, and it will send a feed to the computers here in the base. We'll know beforehand the next time the hacker tries to strike."

Lance and Jason grabbed their gear, which included their new weapons, earpieces, hoodies, and the motion sensors and camera. The warehouse was not far from campus, and they had discussed walking but drove to a nearby parking lot for several reasons. One being they wanted to make a quicker getaway if they were found. The other was they thought two men walking around with a spear and sword could raise, at the very least, a slight suspicion if they were seen.

They parked in a lot behind the warehouse and walked to the backdoor. Lance stayed beside the door while Jason crept next to a boarded-up window. Jason pried a board back and tried to look inside, but it was too dark to see anything. He looked back to Lance and shrugged. Jason walked back to the door while Lance picked the lock, another of the countless ridiculous skills his dad made him learn growing up. Lance got the door open before Jason had even made it back to him, and they were in the warehouse. Lance pressed his sword's button, lighting up a small area around them as they looked through the warehouse, pulling the door closed behind them.

They found a single computer in the corner of the room, but other than that, the warehouse was barren. Lance held the sword above the computer as Jason found a place to set up the camera. As they moved to put the motion sensors at the front door, they heard a noise that forced their hearts to drop: jingling keys in the door. They dashed to separate sides of the warehouse, hoping to stay in the shadows once the door opened. Lance extinguished the light seconds before the soft light from the street drifted into the warehouse.

A solitary person walked into the warehouse, momentarily illuminating the entry of the warehouse before closing the door behind them and sending the room back into darkness. Jason and Lance sat in complete silence, not going as far as to even breathe in order not to risk letting this person know that they were there. A lamp turned on at the computer to show a female sitting at the desk. Lance looked across the room at Jason, who, in the dim light from the lamp, appeared as perplexed as he was. They had anticipated the hacker being a man.

They weren't prepared to fight a girl and weren't sure what to do. Jason took the motion sensors silently out of his pocket and turned them on to wave his hands in front of them. Within seconds, they could hear Taylor's voice in their ears.

"Well, that's not what I had expected. I would have sworn our hacker was one of the fraternity members who just did his hacking elsewhere to keep from being tracked back to the house. I know what you two are thinking, but you still have to question her. Jason, there is a breaker box about halfway between you and the desk. Give Lance a chance to get close to her, and then you shut off the power. Lance, turn on your sword after that and interrogate her. She's already in the corner; just stand between her and the rest of the room with your sword; you shouldn't have to be physical with her. The camera is operated by battery, so I'll still be with you."

Lance looked over at Jason, who motioned for him to start walking. Lance crept forward slowly, careful not to make a sound that might alert the hacker, who was occupied with typing and wasn't looking up from her computer. Once Lance had made it within ten feet, Jason moved toward the breaker box. Lance made it into position and pressed the button. Jason flipped the switch while the hacker was spinning around.

"Who do you work for?" Lance demanded.

"Wh-What?"

"Who do you work for?" Lance growled again.

Another light appeared as Jason's spear added some more light, this one closer to the hacker's head.

"F-F-Fox. I work for Matthew Fox. Please, I'm just trying to pay for my tuition. H-He told me it was for a good cause and that I would be fine. A-All I know is that he needed me to hack the security system on two separate nights for twenty minutes each. He told me he would pay off all my student debt if I did."

"What are you doing here tonight?" Lance barked at her.

"He said there was a mistake with someone else involved last time. He said he would give me some money to start saving with, and when I checked my bank account today, there was fifteen thousand dollars in it."

"When is it?"

"F-Fifteen minutes. I got here early to make sure everything was ready. Fox told me to turn the alarm off five minutes before it was to take place and turn it off five minutes after. He said it should only take ten minutes, but he wanted some extra time to be safe."

Lance stepped back and talked to Taylor.

"Get ready to disable the security system for Gibson. Wait until I get in, and then turn it back on. Jason is going to bring our new friend into the base."

Turning back to Jason, he nodded before turning his sword off and heading for the door. Jason blindfolded the hacker, but left her unbound, and took her to the truck. Lance was already out of sight when Jason got her out the door.

Lance arrived outside of Gibson seventeen minutes later and found the door opened. He walked in and closed the door behind him. "I'm in," he told Taylor, heading to the chem lab.

"There are three of them this time," Taylor told him as he worked his way through the building.

Lance continued through the building. It had been seven minutes since they had gone in. He had three minutes to find them and eight minutes to keep them in the building until the alarm was reset. Lance had walked down the stairwell and was about to turn a corner when three men came around it before he could. Lance struck the first one in the head with the flat end of his sword and then hit him with the hilt to knock him out. One man took off the other way as the other prepared to fight.

Lance struck the fighter twice on the knee, the second one with a jolt of electricity. Lance took off after the other man, leaving the fighter groaning behind him, clutching his knee.

"Four more minutes," Taylor's voice crackled over his earpiece.

"Use the cameras in the building and let me know where he is," Lance growled.

"He just ran past a stairwell. I don't think he knew it was there. Take that and make it to the north exit."

Lance took off up the stairs and sprinted for the exit.

"He just took the main stairwell. He'll be at the door in ten seconds."

Lance arrived in time to see the light leave the thief's eyes as he approached the door. He slid to a stop before running back down the stairs.

"Alarm's back on."

Lance took the exit, setting off the alarm. He jogged over to Baker Hall, where he climbed the fire exit to ensure none of the men left before the campus police arrived. The police were on the scene within two minutes, and not a single thief had made it out yet. Ten minutes later, officers walked back out of the building, but with only two of the thieves.

"Where's the third thief?" Lance asked into the earpiece.

"He's in one of the classrooms. If you can get back in, I can get you to the room."

Lance waited as the officers loaded up the first two thieves. When he was sure no one was watching, he descended the fire escape and walked to the back door. Once in, Taylor came back into his ear.

"He's still in the classroom. Take the stairs up one floor. He's in room two fifty-five."

Lance did as Taylor directed and walked up to room 255. He opened the door to find an empty lecture hall. Lance walked along the wall, searching for a light. After flipping the light on, it took his eyes a moment to adjust. He walked down the aisle as the lights warmed up.

"Where is he?" Lance asked as he made his way to the front of the room without seeing the thief in any of the rows.

"I don't know. I have cameras in the halls, but there's nothing in the classrooms."

Lance walked up the steps onto the stage and walked to the desk off to one side. As he walked in front of the desk, he was struck in the leg, causing him to fall on one leg. The thief tried to run as Lance was on a knee, but Lance backhanded a swing with his sword into the thief's shins, sending him sprawling onto the stage as well. Lance leapt to his feet and hobbled over to the thief struggling to stand. Lance hit him across the back with the sword to send him back to the ground.

Lance grabbed the thief and made him stand. Lance marched him back to the front door with his sword in the thief's back. He shoved him out into the clearing where the officers were still gathered and sank back into the building. He heard officers enter the building right as the door to the stairwell closed. He ran to the top floor as fast as he could and found the fire exit.

"Okay, Taylor, I'm at the top. Is the alarm off?"

"It should be," Taylor responded. "You need to risk it, though, because they're closing in quick."

Lance opened the door and stepped out onto the escape, pulling himself up onto the roof before lying down, panting.

"They're still searching the building for you. Jason was able to find the frequency they're using on their walkie-talkies, and they seem pretty determined to find you. You might want to get comfortable because it could be a while."

"Copy that," Lance responded as he sat the sword down next to him and stretched out.

He sat silently for over an hour, waiting for the last patrol car to finally pull out. Taylor sent the all-clear that he could return to the base safely, and Lance slowly stood and descended the fire escape to begin his short walk to the base.

FIFTEEN

Lance didn't get back to the base until two-thirty in the morning. He hadn't expected the campus police to spend so much time searching for him. *Do they see me as the bad guy? Are we not trying to do the same thing? Keep the campus safe? Or are they just unhappy about being shown up by someone in a hood? Either way, the job just got that much harder going forward*, Lance thought to himself. *Just what I need.*

Lance walked into the base to find a makeshift room in one corner. The campus police issue could wait.

"We didn't want her to know where she was, but we also didn't want to leave her blindfolded since we weren't sure how long you would be gone," Jason explained with a shrug as Lance joined the two at the computer.

"There are two chairs in there, and a lamp is already set up. We'll shut the lights off and let you interrogate her."

Lance acknowledged what they said with a single nod before returning to where the room was set up. "Room" was too generous to describe what he was walking into. All it was were a few of Jason's sheets thrown around the squat rack and salmon ladder. Lance had his sword with him and waited until the lights were off to turn it on. He stepped into the room and turned the lamp on, allowing his sword to go dark once the light was on. The hacker squinted as the light turned on but didn't react other than that. Lance stood inside the sheet and watched her as she adjusted to the light. Brown hair, brown eyes, and a tan still strong from spring break. She wore a light blue Franklin University sweatshirt and black yoga pants.

"What's your name?" Lance asked, sitting down behind the lamp.

"Hannah. What's yours?"

"I'm the White Knight. Why were you hacking into the campus's security system?"

"That doesn't sound like much of a name. Pretty generic if you ask me. What's your real name?"

She seemed much calmer than she did at the warehouse.

Jason and Taylor coddled her too much, Lance thought, shaking his head as he continued the interrogation.

"That's not important. Why were you hacking into campus security?"

"Let me guess. Adam? Ben? Chris? Derek? Eli?"

"Why were you hacking the system?" Lance asked again, beginning to become agitated.

"I think it's hardly fair that you know my name, but I don't know yours. Fred? George? Herman? Isaac? Jack? Kyle?"

"Enough! Either you can tell me what I want to know, and we let you go, or I force you to tell me what I want to know, and then we drop you off at the police station. And trust me," he said, alighting his sword in electricity, "I can be very persuasive."

"Fine," she answered, staring at the sword, deciding not to push him any further. "Like I told you earlier, Matthew Fox paid me to hack into the system. He paid off all my student debt and gave me an extra fifteen thousand. Considering the debt I'm in, I didn't think twice. I have no idea what his plans are, nor why he chose me. I don't really care, either."

"Wait, Matthew Fox? Like the CEO of Fox Industries, Matthew Fox?"

"That's the one."

"Why would a man with his resources need a student hacker or the fraternity?"

"No clue. He told me very little. All he told me was what he wanted me to do and how much he would pay me for doing it."

"How did he contact you?"

"He came to my house the first time. He called me yesterday to ask me to work one more night for him."

"Where is your house?"

"Why do you need to know that?"

"For a couple of reasons. One is that we're not just going to let you walk out of here. We're going to blindfold you again and take you home. The second is that we may need to talk to you again and we need to know where to find you."

"In case one of you wants to come pick me up for a date?" she asked, looking at where Lance's voice was coming from behind the lamp and then past the sheets toward the computers where Jason and Taylor had been earlier.

"No. What do you know about the 'professor' that has been working with the fraternity?"

"Absolutely nothing. All I know is what buildings needed security turned off and when. I didn't ask any questions. Above my pay grade. I've truly told you everything I know. I didn't even know there was a fraternity or professor involved. Can I go home now? It's late, and I have class in the morning."

"Sure, but we need one other thing from you before we take you home. You're going to give us Fox's phone number."

"I can't give you that! He'll know it was me!" she said.

Her eyes widened as the first trace of fear entered her voice.

"It wasn't a question. We're getting his number from you. I'm sure people in the fraternity have it as well."

She shook her head violently but handed her phone over silently as Lance's sword lit up again. Lance slid the phone out of the room and waited as Taylor pulled the number. Seconds later, Taylor reached back through the sheet and handed him the phone. Lance stood and walked to Hannah. He put the phone in her hand and picked up the bandanna from where she had left it after taking it off. He gently tied it around her head and helped her to her feet.

"Get the lights," he commanded softly as he walked Hannah through the sheets. He led her through the doors and to the truck.

Hannah told him where the house was starting from the student union. Lance let her out and told her to wait thirty seconds before removing the blindfold. He watched her in his mirror as he drove away, and when he turned the corner, her blindfold was still on.

The three sat around Taylor's computer in silence. It was now four-thirty in the morning at the base, and they each had classes on Friday. Jason finally broke the silence, looking from Lance to Taylor and back again.

"So, we're done, right? That's what we're all thinking? It's not like we can fight a billionaire with just the three of us. We're not even sure what his plan is, much less how to stop it. This is where this ends? Maybe not protecting the campus, but definitely fighting this battle, right?"

"We know it involves the widespread use of drugs that make people faster and stronger than God or nature intended them to be. That's a pretty good start to understanding his plan."

"Taylor's right," Lance added. "We know enough that we, at least I, can't throw in the towel now. You say we don't know the plan, so I'm going to go figure it out. Tomorrow night, after Taylor's party, I'm going to talk to Fox."

"You're kidding, right? When exactly are you planning on leaving? I only ask because I doubt I'll have enough time to explain to you every reason why this is the worst idea you've ever had if you're leaving tomorrow night. Maybe if you gave me a month, but even that is pushing it." Jason shook his head, cocking it to the side as he continued. "Seriously, Lance, do you even hear yourself? Your entire plan is to just waltz on over to one of the most powerful men in the country to have a chat about him creating drugs that make men super strong and super fast, a drug he already has access to himself, mind you, to tell him what? To stop? Make sure you say please, or he may not even consider it." Jason lifted his palms sarcastically, shaking his head again. "Not only is he a billionaire with plenty of resources at his disposal, but he also served in the army for a five-year tour of duty. It would be one thing if he was some old man, but he's not. He's what? Fifteen years older than we are? And he might have already tested these drugs on himself? You're out of your mind."

"Jason's right, Lance. Your whole plan can't consist of going to his house and confronting him. You need to be smarter about this."

"I can't sit back and do nothing!" Lance slapped the table. "We know he plans on making more of these drugs, and then what? No one will be able to stop him. If I don't try now, then no one will. It may not be a good plan, but it's the only course of action I see to take. Someone has to stop this, and we're in the best place to do so."

"Why don't we, I don't know, tell the police? Or the FBI? I understand how going solo works well to protect the campus, but this just got a whole lot bigger than that," Jason answered, his voice rising.

"They won't believe anything we tell them. You said so yourself that he's one of the most powerful men in the country. They're not going to take my word over his. And let's not forget that we took the frat thief and dropped him off on their front porch, and they let him go a few hours later with no charges. If they wouldn't help us deal with the fraternity, they're definitely not helping us with Fox. And what do you suppose we tell the FBI? 'Hello, I'm a vigilante in Missouri, and I have information about how Matthew Fox is creating an army of super soldiers?' They'd laugh us out of the building if they even let us get that far. No, this has to be done by us."

"Taylor, help me out here. You can't think this is a smart idea."

"It's definitely not a smart idea."

"Thank you!" Jason gestured with his hands at Taylor while widening his eyes at Lance.

"But Lance may be right," Taylor added hesitantly. "There aren't always smart options; sometimes all you're left with is deciding which choice is the least dumb. All of our options have the same floor, with Fox creating a super army. That's the worst-case scenario, no matter what we do. The best case is not much different if we do nothing. We may not have much of a shot if we try, but at least there's a chance. The risk is basically the same with either choice. The reward is significantly different with us taking action."

"I can't believe you're actually agreeing with him. Aren't you supposed to be the sensible one?"

"I'm trying to be, but you're not listening."

"We don't even know that he's making an army or what he would do if he had one. Sure, it's probably something not great, but there's a chance that he has some altruistic motive for these drugs. Taylor, are you telling me there wouldn't be huge benefits for the medical community if he figures out these drugs? And the risk in going is not the same as not going because one of those could very likely end with Lance dying while the other has no chance of that!"

Lance stood, stretching. "Look, I've made my decision. I'm driving to Duncan tomorrow night. You can help or stay out of it. That choice is yours, and I understand either way, but I'm going. I'm also going to bed now to get as much rest as I can before then. Don't worry about seeing if I'm up for class; I'm not going to them. I'll see you guys tomorrow." With that, Lance turned from the computer and left for the apartment.

Lance didn't wake until one in the afternoon the next day. He walked into the living room and found a note on the bar. *Come to the base when you get up. We've got something for you.* Lance walked into the kitchen and made a sandwich he bit into as he walked out to his truck. He pulled up to the storage unit and walked in, unsure what to expect. *If they intend to try to talk me out of going tonight,* he thought, opening the door, *this conversation will not be pretty.* As he entered the unit, he was met with another sheet-laden case.

"Am I getting a new sword?"

"Better," Jason called out from under his workstation.

He stood, brushing the dust off his pants. As he did so, Taylor came over from his table to meet Lance and Jason at the case.

"Look, I still think this is crazy, but I'm not letting you go in there without a fighting chance. I've been working on this more or less since I found you unconscious outside the library, but I stayed up all night finishing it so you could use it tonight." Jason reached for the sheet, pulling it off to reveal the suit he had built for him.

"There are three layers to the suit," he continued as Lance marveled at what was in front of him, "all of them are white to go with your new name. The first is a body suit. It will allow you a full range of motion, but it gives very little protection. It's mainly there to wick sweat and keep the rest of the suit from cutting you up or chafing. The second layer is the foundation of a suit I made from a new metal material I made that is stronger than Kevlar. It's a light layer so that you can still move around. I wouldn't try to get shot if I were you, but if you do, this layer will keep it from killing you, though it would still be really painful. Each part of the third layer is separate. There are two pieces on each arm, and the forearm plate sticks out to protect the elbow. Two pieces on each leg, and both pieces have an overhang to protect the knee. These are all made of the same material but thicker. It's a light material, but with all of it combined, it's definitely heavier than the sweatshirt you've been wearing, but the amount of protection it will offer you more than makes up for the weight. I also made you custom white boots, but while they are still protected, they aren't made of the same material. You wouldn't be able to walk, much less run, in boots made of that. Same thing with the gloves. They're padded and protected, but you wouldn't be able to fight if they were armored.

Your torso will be covered by a vest that's connected at the shoulders. There is a clip underneath your arms and then a loop on both lower corners in the front and back. Your belt will come equipped with a sheath to hold your sword. All of this top layer is lined with rubber, so you can place your sword on the suit and light the whole thing up if you need to. Lastly"—he grinned, reaching for the top of the case—"we have your helmet. This is also the thicker metal. It only has other materials as needed for its capabilities. There's a built-in headset that connects you to Taylor and me and a camera that will send us a live feed as you fight. There is a soft pad on the piece that runs along your jaw to keep it from becoming too uncomfortable. The white visor will cover your eyes and the rest of the upper half of your face to keep your identity concealed, but it shouldn't affect your vision while fighting. Getting used to it may be an adjustment, especially when running and climbing, but we think it's worth it."

"Isn't the whiteness of it a little counterproductive? It will be hard to sneak around in this."

"That's the point. You're no longer 'the vigilante,' Lance. You are the White Knight. You've become a symbol. You want people to know that you're out there. You can still be careful, obviously, but when you arrive, you want the victim and the aggressor to know who just arrived. You're the embodiment of hope to this campus,

Lance. Whether you like it or not, people look to you for that. You know as well as anyone that our campus was messed up before the White Knight arrived. We've been one of the most violent universities for years, and you changed that. People need to know you're out there. And they will. Your days of hiding in the dark are over. You're stepping into the light now. And now that you have Taylor monitoring the campus, you won't need to patrol the same way. We've also worked together to create an actual symbol for you that you can see on the vest." Jason pointed to a black area on the center of the chest piece. "It's a white shield except for a black outline around the shield so that it contrasts with the rest of your suit. In the middle of the shield is a white knight, as in the chess piece. What do you think?" he asked with a huge smile.

"I think you two did fantastic. What does it say at the bottom of the shield?"

"I added that," Taylor answered. "I had the same reservations about your suit being white. After Jason explained his idea for the suit to me, I remembered a Latin phrase I had heard in my class: 'Dum Spiro, Spero.' It translates as, 'While I breathe, I hope.' I thought it fit well with the message we're trying to send." Taylor shrugged and gave him a sheepish smile.

"It definitely does, Taylor. It's a good addition. But what about Fox? Do I want him to know I'm there tonight?"

"You're going to his house to confront him. If you don't want him to know you're there, then I'm even more confused as to why you're going," Jason sighed. "Look, he's going to know you're there before you get to him. I guarantee that. You may as well be wearing something less amateurish and more functional than a hoodie."

"I guess I'll take it," Lance said with a smile as he stepped up to the case to get a closer inspection of his new suit.

chapter

SIXTEEN

Jason and Lance's job for the day was to keep Taylor occupied so that Gwen and Hailey could put together his surprise party for that night. Gwen had been planning it for a month, awkwardly changing subjects every time he approached to prevent him from finding out. Roughly a week into their planning, Hailey asked Jason if he could help pick up the decorations before the party, not realizing that Taylor was in the kitchen. She tried to backtrack, but the damage had been done. Taylor quickly agreed not to say anything to Gwen and to act surprised when he showed up to the party after Hailey told him what would happen to him if he didn't.

Occupying him wouldn't have been difficult as Taylor was plenty busy on his own that day trying to get everything ready for Lance and Jason's thirty-minute trip north to Duncan that night to confront Fox. Lance's suit had simplified Taylor's work considerably. The multiple cameras in the helmet would prove even more critical tonight since Taylor didn't have access to the cameras in Fox's house. Still, Taylor wanted to check and recheck every bit of tech Jason had installed and make sure the connection with his system was seamless.

Jason was at work preparing for that night as well. He was charging Lance's sword while also maintaining the sword's body with his whetstone. Jason was clueless about what Lance may come across that night, and he wanted to ensure that Lance's sword was as good as he could. Jason still wasn't sure about the mission. He didn't possess nearly the confidence in Lance as Lance himself did, nor did he have Taylor's ability to see risking Lance as the lesser of the evils. All he had to go on was faith that his two friends knew what they were doing. He had the smallest part of the plan; he was nothing but the getaway driver, but he was still terrified of the drive to Duncan with Lance and even more terrified that the drive back would be without him.

Lance had the most significant job that night but the least to do to prepare for what was to come. He tried to lift weights, but Taylor stopped him so he didn't tire himself out. He tried to spar with Jason, but Jason told him he was too busy working on his gear, and Taylor again reminded him not to tire himself. So Lance paced the room with nothing to think about except for the fate that awaited him that night, a topic that he desperately wanted to avoid until he was in Duncan. After thirty minutes of pacing silently, Lance checked his phone to see that it was only three in the afternoon. With four hours remaining before the party, Lance couldn't take not doing anything much longer.

"I'm going to go see if Gwen needs any help."

"You sure that's a good idea?" Taylor asked, looking up from his computer.

"Yeah, isn't she still mad at you?" Jason added, keeping his eyes focused on his work.

"Yes, but I'm planning on confronting a man who could very well kill me tonight, and I would rather not die with Gwen not speaking to me. She said she would talk to me at the party, but I'm hoping I can get away with showing up early if I offer to help."

"Good luck with that. We'll see you over there. And remember, you and Jason are leaving the party at eleven, and you're going to be fighting a man who might be on some sort of super-strength drug and could probably beat you without any. In case you needed another reason to avoid anything impairing you tonight."

"I appreciate your optimism, Taylor. I'll see you guys tonight."

Lance parked his truck outside of Gwen and Hailey's house. He killed the engine and took a deep breath before taking the keys out of the ignition and walking to the door. Knocking three times, he waited for an answer. It was Hailey.

"Do you need any help setting things up?"

"Yes. I have to go get the food, and Gwen is trying to set up the decorations by herself, but there is too much left for her to do it alone. I know you two are fighting, but we really need your help. I'll be back in an hour tops. Whatever you do, don't let her make you leave. Believe me, she'll definitely try," she said while leaving him a pat on the shoulder.

"Almost as optimistic as Taylor," Lance muttered as he walked into the living room.

"Hailey said you could use some help," Lance hollered out as he walked into the living room.

Gwen came out of the kitchen and glared at him. "I would rather work alone," she declared, returning to the kitchen.

Lance followed a step before stopping and calling out.

"Hailey told me you were behind and could use some help. And not to brag or anything, but I'm pretty good at housework. When you're an only child with two workaholics for parents, you become pretty good at that sort of stuff."

She came back out. "I told you I'd rather work alone." She turned back to the kitchen before her face softened, and she turned back to him. "I do need help, though. The living room needs to be cleaned and vacuumed. You can help as long as you stay quiet." She spoke softly as she headed back into the kitchen.

"That's going to be pretty difficult if I'm vacuuming." She poked her head out of the kitchen to glare at him again, after which Lance didn't say another word until he had completely vacuumed, dusted, and otherwise cleaned the living room.

Once he had vacuumed the living room, he went to the kitchen. Gwen looked at the door as he walked in and stopped putting her decorations up, still standing on her chair.

"You can go hang some of our decorations on the back porch now. They're on the patio table."

"I thought I'd help you in here. We need to talk."

"I told you we would talk at Taylor's party. It's not his party yet."

"Not completely true. You told me we would talk on Taylor's birthday, which is today. You said nothing about having to wait until the party."

"Lance, I don't have time to fight with you over this right now. I have work to do to get the house ready. Either you can help, or you can leave."

"Well, that's convenient because I don't plan on fighting." Lance picked up a banner and put it up over the door. "I'm really sorry for how I acted after what happened. I wasn't being a good friend, but Jason and Taylor talked to me, and I've been working on it. I just want to be us again."

"And how do you suggest we do that, Lance? You weren't there with me that night like I needed you to be, but I can't blame you for what happened. But there is no excuse for you abandoning me in the aftermath. The person I needed more than anyone else was you. You were the person I was closest to and had always been able to lean on. Who was it that got the emergency call from the hospital? My roommate? My cousin? No. It was you. And you repaid that trust by distancing yourself from me and pushing me away because of your guilt. It's not easy to just forget something like that, Lance. Believe me, I've been trying."

"You're right. I'm not asking you to forget it. It happened, and I don't think you could possibly understand how much I hate having hurt you like that. I am so sorry for abandoning you the way I did. I was trying to work through my own feelings, and I let that hurt you, and that's not okay. I put my needs over yours when you needed me to be there for you like you've always been there for me. I was selfish. You have every right to be upset with me. All I'm asking is for you to remember the twenty-one-plus years that came before that. I'm asking you to remember all that we've been through together. Are you thinking about it? Now, decide which version of me you think I'm more likely to resemble going forward."

"I know which person is more likely to show up going forward, but that doesn't change the one that didn't show up when I needed it. I need more time."

"More time will do nothing but drive us further apart. Being apart is what got us into this in the first place. Don't you think then that being together would do us more good? I've had a lot on my mind lately, but no matter how much I had to do, I never stopped thinking about you and wanting to be with you. This time we've spent apart isn't helping because all you can think about when you think of me is how I acted for those months when I hurt you. I'm better now. I'm better than I was the past few months. I'm better than I was at any time before last December, too. But I can't show you that as long as you refuse to talk to me."

"Okay."

"Okay?"

"Okay. I've missed you, too. And everything isn't better or back to normal. I understand that what happened affected you, too, but that doesn't make it okay. I can forgive you, but it's going to take some time before I can trust you again, Lance. I can't just forget what happened. We're going to have to have more conversations before we are even close to being like we used to be, and those conversations are going to be uncomfortable."

"One hundred percent. I want to have those conversations with you. I know it's going to be uncomfortable and even painful at times, but it can't be as painful as not talking to you."

Her face softened as she stepped down off the chair.

"We still have a lot to do before the party tonight, and a lot of these decorations would be easier to put up with two sets of hands. Let's start on the porch."

"Together?"

"Together," she said with a smile.

Hailey returned with the groceries to find the house empty. She laid the bags on the kitchen table and turned to go back to the car to get more when she heard laughter coming from the back porch. She walked to the glass door and was surprised to find it coming from Gwen as she and Lance were putting decorations up together.

"You two better?"

Gwen and Lance looked at each other.

"We're getting there," Gwen answered with a smile.

"Good. I miss hanging out as a group with Jason and Taylor. And if that means having Locke back in my life, I guess I'll take it."

People began showing up as seven approached. Lance found himself in his familiar party spot in the corner as the house filled up. Unfortunately, Jason had yet to arrive with Taylor, and Gwen was busy hosting, so he was on his own for now. He stopped Hailey as she walked by.

"Does Jason have a reason for bringing Taylor, or is he just supposed to convince Taylor to come here for nothing?"

"Actually, I'm just using this party as an excuse for Jason to run an errand for me. My cousin is moving to Duncan from Oklahoma, and he's going to stay with us until he finds a place up there. I called J earlier, and I'm having him and Taylor pick him up from the airport for me. I'll talk to you later. I need to go help Gwen in the kitchen right now."

As she left, another girl came and took her place. Lance knew he had seen her before but had no idea where. She was as tall as Hailey with shoulder-length blonde hair, but Lance couldn't seem to place her.

"Have we met before?" she asked as Hailey walked away.

"I don't believe so. I'm Lance." He reached out his hand.

She shook it and also her head.

"Are you sure? You look so familiar, and I know that I've heard your voice somewhere before. I think we've met."

"Well, then, I apologize for not remembering you. Maybe we had a class together? What's your name?"

"Ashley. Ashley Adair. I doubt we've had a class together. I'm just a freshman this year."

Lance's heart skipped a beat as he realized where he had seen this girl before. He hadn't masked his voice well that night, and she seemed a little too confident that she knew who he was.

"Then I can't think of where we would have met," he said, trying to recover. "Who are you here with? I know most of Taylor's friends are upperclassmen."

"Hailey Hall invited me. She interviewed me for a story a few weeks ago, and we've become friends since then. Gwen, too. Do you go to many sporting events on campus? I'm on the soccer team, and we end up going to most of them. Maybe there?"

"I haven't gone to any games since my sophomore year so that probably isn't it."

Ashley shook her head, disappointed. "I know we've met before. I just cannot remember where."

"That is strange." Lance was looking away as Gwen's voice cut through the crowd.

"He's here!" she yelled as everyone prepared to surprise Taylor.

Much to Lance's relief, Ashley left to join a group behind the couch. The door opened, and the house erupted as Taylor walked in.

Taylor did his best to act surprised, and while he may not have fooled everyone, judging by her grin, Gwen believed him, and that was all that really mattered.

Taylor walked around the party, thanking everyone for coming while Jason unloaded the car with Hailey's cousin. Lance walked out to the car to see Jason.

"Do you need any help?"

Jason stood from out of the trunk. "Yeah, if you help, we should be able to make it all in one trip."

A man came around from the other side of the car wearing a blue and orange checkered flannel shirt with his jeans. "Hi," he said, "I'm Sam Hall. I'm going to be living here for a few weeks while I look for a place up in Duncan." He greeted Lance with a giant smile and an enormous outstretched hand.

He was darker complected, his Native American heritage even more visible than Hailey's. He was a couple of inches taller than Lance but just shy of Jason's height, though he was every bit as muscular as Jason, if not more so. His long black hair was piled on top of his head in a bun.

"Lance," he responded, shaking Sam's hand.

After they had introduced themselves, Sam grabbed four of his bags and walked toward the house. When he was out of earshot, Lance grabbed Jason by the arm and began talking.

"I think someone might know who I am."

"Well, this is a party full of people to celebrate Taylor's birthday, so it's inevitable that at least some of them will know who you are, even if you've been even more of a hermit the last few months," he said, picking up three bags of his own.

"I think someone knows who the White Knight is."

That stopped Jason. He looked around to make sure no one could hear him.

"Who?"

"Ashley, a girl Hailey invited. She's one of the people I had saved. She's the one who came up with the name. She came by, started talking to me, and said she thought she recognized me but couldn't figure out from where."

"I'm sure it will be fine if she doesn't remember where she met you. We'll talk to Taylor about it later. Help me get these bags into the house. Sam packed a ton."

The party started to die by ten-thirty that night, and Lance and Jason were both jittery. By ten-forty-five, they couldn't take it anymore and began to leave.

"You're already leaving?" Gwen asked as she saw them leaving.

"Unfortunately," Jason answered, "we both have something we need to take care of. We'll try to come by tomorrow to help with the cleanup."

Lance gave Gwen a long hug, and Jason kissed Hailey as they left and got into Jason's car. They stopped by the base to grab all of their equipment and were on the road to Duncan. They sat silently the whole trip, neither wanting to talk about what could happen tonight. Neither able to think of anything else.

SEVENTEEN

Lance left Jason at the car without a word said between the two. They both knew what Lance was walking into, and putting words to it seemed hollow, so a simple nod was all they exchanged as Lance stepped out of the truck and onto the sidewalk. They parked two blocks away so that if something went wrong, Jason could get away unseen. No reason for both to get caught.

Duncan, specifically the wealthy area where Fox lived, was much better lit than the college campus at Franklin. He still made the two-block trips without being seen, but he had to put more effort into it than he was accustomed to, sticking to the shadows lying under trees as the occasional car would drive past. The white suit he was wearing wasn't helping matters, either. Luckily, the area was empty during those ten minutes. He stood across the street from Fox's house, taken aback by the size of the home. "House," he realized, didn't do Fox's home justice, though, as it more closely resembled a castle than anything else. Lance would have thought he had walked back in time and crossed the ocean if there had been a moat and spires. He took one last deep breath and crossed the street.

Once across the street, Lance skirted along the castle's boundary wall. Fox's grounds had even more lighting than the street. After finding a dimmer area, Lance climbed the wall and fell to the ground with hardly a sound as he landed on the grass. Lance didn't move as he took in his surroundings. Thirty feet remained between the castle and himself, and while it appeared clear, he wasn't so sure. He crept forward, stopping every few steps to survey his surroundings. After continuing at this glacial pace, he finally arrived at the castle's wall. Seeing no one, Lance climbed up to a second-story balcony using the wall's rough exterior. He leapt onto the balcony, hand reaching to his sheath, but found no one in the area. He reached for the handle to push into the castle's interior before hearing someone say his name. He unsheathed his sword and sharply made a one-hundred-eighty-degree turn but found no one with him on the balcony. His name was spoken again, and Lance breathed a sigh of relief once he realized Taylor was speaking in his helmet.

"Lance, why are you swinging the sword?"

"I hadn't expected to hear your voice. I thought someone was behind me."

"Hold on"—Jason's voice joined Taylor's in the helmet—"not only did you think that Fox had some sort of patrol on lookout for you, but you also expected them to know your real name? Don't you think you're getting a little ahead of yourself as far as just how many people are aware of the White Knight's existence?"

"I'm a little on edge right now, Jason, so forgive me for being a bit paranoid. What were you trying to tell me, Taylor?" Lance asked as he sheathed his sword.

"Just that I'm on now. I'll be pretty useless to you tonight. I have no plans of the house to guide you, and there are no cameras at my disposal other than the ones on your suit, so you're on your own."

"Well, thank you for breaking radio silence to deliver that pressing report. If it's all the same to you, I'm going to go back to trying to find Fox now." *And try to keep from getting killed,* Lance thought to himself as he, once again, reached for the handle and then stepped through the doorway into the castle as he opened the balcony door.

Lance froze as he stepped into the castle from the balcony. No alarms went off. No army of security guards was rushing him. He was inside Fox's home, and he had yet to come across any indication that anyone knew he was there. He crept across the room, avoiding the dust-covered bed and wardrobe, to the dimly lit door. Once there, Lance opened the door slowly and looked into the hallway. Still nothing. The hallway was even darker than the room was, causing Lance to go even slower to ensure he didn't run over something that would alert Fox of his presence any sooner than necessary. He made his way down the hall with a faint light leaking in from behind a door at the end of it.

Lance approached the door, leaning on the wall next to it as he arrived, his ear next to the door. He ceased breathing for a moment, trying to discern if any noises were coming from the room. After thirty seconds with no sound but that of his resumed breathing, Lance opened the door with one hand and grasped the hilt of his sword with the other. The door opened to reveal a brightly lit room, causing Lance to squint. As his eyes adjusted, he moved forward through the kitchen he found himself in. It was by far the largest kitchen he had ever been in, and at the end, he found it was connected to four other rooms. Two of the doors had no light coming from under them, so he ignored those for now. He reached for the handle on the right and found it was locked. The left door opened into a large walk-in pantry with no exit. He turned his attention back to the first door and radioed Taylor.

"How do I get into this room? The door is locked, and who knows how long it will take me to find another way in. If there even is another way in. Are you two seeing anything I'm not?"

"Did you take anything other than your sword?"

"No. I didn't expect to need much else."

"Well, unless Jason has any ideas for how to use your sword to open it, your best bet is to knock it down. Jason?"

"I don't know how the sword would really help. The electric current wouldn't do much right now. You could knock."

Lance turned the headset off without replying to Jason. He walked back through the kitchen to the door he had entered through and reentered the hallway. He would prefer not to knock down a door, both because he didn't want to alert everyone in the castle that he was there, and he would rather not give Fox more reason to try and hurt him. He started with the first door on the left side of the hall. It opened into a restroom with no other way in or out. He tried the next door on the left. It was locked. As were the next three. Lance came to the last door in the hallway, and this one opened to another hallway. Lance walked the entire hallway, not coming to a single door until the end of the hall.

He opened this one to find himself in a bedroom, the first room he had come across that looked as if it had been lived in. A pair of shoes sat next to the perfectly made bed, a suit was hanging from a hook on the closet door, and the desk off to the side was covered in an array of papers, the only part of the room that wasn't orderly. Lance carefully walked across the room to the door on the opposite side, where light entered the room from the gap at the bottom of the door. He slowly turned the knob. It was locked.

Great. He walked to the other door in the room and stepped out onto the balcony it led to. Lance looked over at the next room and could see no one in it, though he could see the lights were on, and it appeared to be a study or home library. It was definitely the room he was trying to reach.

"Great," he mumbled to himself. "The one room in this entire castle without a balcony is the one I can't get into."

Lance returned to the bedroom to sit on the edge of the bed, slightly wrinkling the perfectly made comforter. He turned his headset back on to talk to Jason and Taylor again.

"As far as I can tell, there is no one in the castle besides me and whoever is in that room, which, I assume, is Fox. I can't think of any other way to get in without breaking a door down. Please tell me one of you have an idea."

"I still think your best bet is to kick the door down."

"And I still think that if you knock, someone will open the door, and you won't end up hurting yourself before you even face Fox."

"Is this a joke to you, Jason?"

"Your situation? No, but your plan? Definitely. He's a billionaire. Do you really think his doors, which he's taken the time to lock while alone in his castle, are just going to fall over because you lower your shoulder? Because you have grit or determination? This isn't a comic book, Lance. You can knock, or you can break through the window. You're not going to be able to knock that door over."

Lance walked back to the balcony, gazing across the gap between the balcony and the window.

"Taylor, can you figure out how far the window is from me from the suit cameras? I need an estimate on how far I'll need to jump to decide if I can make it."

"It's an eight-foot jump from the point nearest to the house. There's a small ledge you can grab onto and stand on before entering. Be aware, though, that it's a twenty-foot drop if you miss it, and there's a concrete patio below you here."

"Plus, that suit was built with protection in mind more than your jumping. You can still probably make it, but you need to factor in the added weight before you jump. It won't protect you from a twenty-foot drop onto concrete as it would from body blows."

"I don't really have another option. As much as I hate admitting it, Jason, you're right. That door isn't falling."

Lance climbed on top of the balcony's railing and prepared to launch himself. He checked his sword to ensure it would stay when he jumped and adjusted his helmet. Shaking his arms, he took two quick deep breaths. *Here goes nothing.*

He leapt, wind racing in under his helmet, as he fell through the air. He caught the ledge with his right hand but missed with his left as his body swung away from the ledge. Dangling and barely able to hold himself up with his gloved hand, he threw his left hand up to grasp onto the ledge. He pulled himself up onto the narrow ledge and sat, taking a moment to rest as he panted after his jump.

Lance sat there until he finally got his breathing under control. He slowly stood on the ledge, drawing his sword as he did so.

Swinging the sword, he leapt through the window as the glass shattered all around him. He landed in a fighting stance, his eyes darting around the room, looking for enemies attacking as the shards of glass rained down around him. All he found, though, was a single man sitting in a leather-bound chair, reading a book.

"Take a seat. I've been dying to meet the White Knight, and I've been expecting you for some time now."

EIGHTEEN

"Go on," Fox said, gesturing to another chair to his left as he sat the book down, "have a seat."

Lance didn't move. He stood with his sword still held out in front of him.

"Go ahead." Fox chuckled and smiled at him. "I only want to talk to you. I think we just have a classic misunderstanding on our hands." Lance hesitantly sat. "I've been waiting for you to come since you started prioritizing the Kappas. Once you caught Hannah, I knew it couldn't be long." He took a sip from his glass. "I was curious as to how you would get into the room. The locked doors were just a test, a personality test, if you will. See, I would have pegged you more of a break-the-door-down kind of man, so a daring jump to the window was a pleasant surprise. Shows you're more than just power. There's agility and athleticism to what you do as well. Though, you could have saved some time and risk by just knocking. I'm sorry, I haven't even introduced myself. My name is Matthew Fox."

The man stood and extended his hand.

"I know who you are," Lance answered quietly without moving.

Lance got a much better look at the man he had first seen in the shadows of the courtyard. He had short brown hair graying on the sides and a pair of dark brown eyes. He was more muscular than Lance remembered. It was easier to see the muscle definition in the T-shirt and jeans he was wearing now than in the suit he had first seen him in. His strong jaw came to a dimple on his chin.

"I see," Fox responded unfazed, sitting back down in his chair. Once he made himself comfortable, he continued. "Then tell me more about yourself since you already know who I am. I find you incredibly interesting. I've been following your story in your college papers. I may not have gone to Franklin, but I have given considerable donations in the past and like to skim through the paper occasionally. The story of a masked hero, your story, of course, stood out. What kind of person does it take to decide to become above the law and dish out vigilante justice?"

Lance did not respond. Fox allowed the silence to draw on while he took another drink from his glass. Lance looked around the room at the different animal heads strewn about the walls. He was as content as Fox to let the silence remain.

Fox broke the silence.

"Are you trying to keep your identity a secret? To save those you love and whatnot? Admirable. Kind of pointless, seeing as how easy it would be for me to uncover your identity if I so pleased, but admirable nonetheless. No doubt, a key to you becoming a vigilante is this desire to protect others. That's telling in itself. So, we move on. Please tell me why you've traveled from Franklin to visit me at my humble abode," he said with a smile, stretching his arms out to gesture at his house.

"Why are you attacking my campus with your drug ring?"

"Attacking? I am in no way attacking your campus. That's why I've been so confused about why a hooded man has been trying to disrupt my philanthropy on campus. None of my supplements are being used on your campus. As far as your campus is concerned, this is all that is happening: I have hired a fraternity, one in which I am the sole donor, to begin with, to work with an esteemed professor to create a new drug for me in return for a very generous donation to their house. Dr. Jacobsen is one of the leading minds in this particular field of genetics, and he happens to be a professor at Franklin. I provided funding and manpower, and he gets to do research without the bureaucratic oversight that can tie the hands of great minds. Your campus has nothing to worry about. I'm not putting any drugs into your campus, only money."

"If you're not trying to sell the drugs on campus, then what are they for?"

"Excellent question. I hope that once I explain my vision, you will understand there is no reason for you to continue antagonizing me and see that we could even make a great team by working together."

Fox stood from his seat and walked to a cabinet to pour himself more to drink. He slowly sipped out of his glass before he paced in front of Lance. After finding a rhythm with his walking, he addressed Lance again.

"I guess I should start with some backstory so you can better understand why I'm going to do this. My father was a wealthy man. He founded this company that I now run. He was a lot of things. Wealthy, powerful, and genius, to name a few. What he was not, though, was caring. He cared for nothing but the bottom line. The poor, the hurting, and the oppressed meant nothing to him. After he passed away, leaving his company to myself, I began giving back diligently to those causes he had overlooked and, in many cases, caused even more harm. Now, as I'm sure you already know, I also care for my country, fighting in the Middle East as a young man who hadn't even attended college yet. It was there that I saw what tragedies wars caused. The gunfights and bombings would kill just as many, if not more, civilians as soldiers. And for what? These wars last years, decimating both sides for a few years of peace before we are back to fighting the very same people."

He walked back to pour himself another glass.

"And do you know why that is? Because men are not afraid of guns. Not as long as they have their own guns. Humans are an incredibly arrogant group. As long as the footing is somewhat equal, we firmly believe that our country or faction will win. So, consequently, we don't take kindly to losing and will seek to redeem ourselves on the battlefield the first chance we get, thus continuing the never-ending cycle of war and violence perpetuated by the powerful people who get to stay safely at home lining their pockets while sending others off to fight their battles. There is only one way for peace to be achieved. And that is to make the battlefield a place of inequality. To bring equality to those who are oppressed, there must be inequality elsewhere. You must balance the scales. Humans aren't fair or equal by their nature. By bringing inequality to war, I will be ending all wars. There will, of course, be challengers at the start, but after defeating those firstcomers, others will realize it is a pointless endeavor. And, once others are afraid to attack my army, the mere threat of my power will keep wars from taking place that don't include me since they know I can and will come to join in fighting both sides. This will give countries the funds to start caring for the less fortunate that surround them since they no longer must worry about pumping money into militaries to fight others."

"And how exactly do you plan on bringing this inequality?"

Fox tilted his glass in Lance's direction as he continued pacing. "That's where my new supplements come into play. The production at Franklin is just a small part of the enterprise. I have other genius professors or scientists working to create new supplements that enhance man's abilities nationwide. Some are at universities, some are at private labs, and others are at newly established think tanks. These supplements will allow me to create super soldiers. Men who can run faster, jump higher, and fight longer than a normal human. They will be harder to take down and harder to defend against at first, and as I continue to perfect my serum, they will become impossible to defeat. My army will be able to win wars quicker and more efficiently than any army this world has ever seen. I will come into the conflict, ensure peace, and retreat to the plains like a modern-day Cincinnatus."

"So, you're just going to start attacking random countries, assuming others won't come to their aid?"

"Nonsense. I have a very clear battle plan. I've been working on it for a while now. I am still putting the finishing touches on the details, but please know I have spent years thinking about this strategically. For obvious reasons, I won't be sharing that plan with you until we are partners, but 'attacking random countries,' as you put it, wouldn't be the plan at all. That would lead to more civilian deaths than what is currently happening. That's not at all the outcome I am looking for. I will be attacking actual militaries that are currently engaged in war, decimating those militaries, and putting the world on notice that these wars won't be tolerated anymore."

"You're going to kill just as many people as you save! How can you justify all the death and oppression you will cause by doing this?"

"Young man, are you familiar with the trolley problem? Have you found time for philosophy in between your," Fox waved a hand toward Lance, "extracurriculars? It will be a temporary setback to a larger solution. Short-term war will lead to long-term peace. That is a tradeoff I am willing to make. Everyone involved will have already signed up to join a war. They knew the risks of that. By killing a few thousand who are in the process of killing others, I will save tens of millions of lives in future wars and billions of lives of people who will now get the resources they need to survive without national security budgets eating into taxpayer money."

"And who are you to choose whether or not to take that tradeoff?"

"I am the man who will have the most powerful army this world has ever seen. I am also that man that will be willing to do what's necessary in order to reset the global economy to focus more on caring for people than killing them."

Lance unsheathed his sword as he made a half circle around Fox. "Then I can't let you get to that point. Whatever your reasons are for doing this, I can't stand by while you kill people."

"Let me point out the irony in a man in a mask who has been doling out justice on his own terms for months telling me that I can't try and do the same," Fox said as he walked to the fireplace and pulled down a cloth-wrapped bundle from the mantle. "I had hoped to convince you to join me. You have proven yourself a valiant fighter. That, along with your clear set of strong morals, would have made you an excellent officer in my army. You would require some training in the more nuanced areas, of course, but nonetheless, I had hoped to recruit you. But if you choose to oppose me, then I will have to dispose of you, no matter how much potential you possess."

After removing the cloth, Fox was left with only his own sword in his hand. He held it in one hand, weighing it before settling into a fighting stance.

Lance lunged at him with his sword, but Fox easily deflected his blow. Lance circled back around, keeping an eye on Fox. Lance feinted a cross swing before following through with a jab, but Fox was ready and knocked that blow away as well. It continued in this manner, with Lance on the attack and Fox dispatching his advances with ease. Fox had yet to attack Lance. Lance tried a combination he had learned in fencing, leaving himself open for a counter to risk catching Fox off guard, but was stopped once more. *He's toying with me.* He continued to leave himself open for counters, but Fox had yet to take advantage of a single opportunity. *Well,* he thought to himself, *you're not the only one with toys.* Knowing he didn't need to worry about Fox countering, Lance made a risky move that allowed him to catch Fox on the hip. Fox yelled out in pain as Lance hit him with his sword activated, sending an electric current into Fox.

Fox jumped back, glaring at Lance, and resting a hand over his burning flesh with his free hand. He walked back in and disarmed Lance in a matter of seconds with three quick moves. Fox hit him across the back with the hilt of his sword, sending him sprawling onto his stomach. Lance stumbled to his feet but wasn't there long before Fox advanced again, swiping at Lance's knee before hitting him across his helmet. Fox rose up and paced to where Lance's sword was and kicked it across the floor to him.

Fox was much quicker than Lance had expected. Stronger as well. For someone his age to be that much quicker than a young man entering his prime was un-nerving. *Maybe he really has already been using his own drugs,* Lance thought to himself.

"Get up," Fox commanded, all remnants of the charismatic man he had been speaking to moments earlier having vanished.

Lance staggered to his feet, where he picked up his sword. Once he was on his feet, Fox engaged him, again disarming him in short order. Fox slashed at his leg again before hitting Lance across the head with the hilt of his sword. Lance collapsed at Fox's feet. Fox walked away, leaving Lance lying on the floor. Fox stopped in front of the fireplace and wrapped the cloth back around his sword before placing it back on his mantle. He walked back to where Lance was still strewn out on the floor and crouched in front of him.

"I apologize for the hostility. Behavior like that is unacceptable for a host. But I was upset at your little party trick. Now, I could kill you. It would be easy. But, regardless of what you may think, I do not find any enjoyment in senseless killing. Your death would be painless for you but would keep me up at night. And, so, I will leave you alive and leave you with this warning. I may not be putting any drugs into your campus, but I will be placing a bomb there for two reasons. One reason is that I don't want there to be any trace of me having been there, and my researcher, who has been leading this project for me, has been called away to handle some other projects I need him working on. Since I don't know exactly what he would need to clean or clear, and I'm certainly not going to trust the kids in that little club he's been using, I am going to make it all a non-factor. The other reason is that for my plan to succeed, I need public opinion fully behind me. This will allow me to come to the aid after a tragedy and donate the funds to rebuild the building, making it even better this time. Maybe I'll even let them name it after me. It's up to you to make sure that no one dies from the bomb, an outcome neither of us wants. You have ten days to ensure no students are in the chemistry building when the bomb goes off a week from Monday."

Fox lifted Lance's helmet off his head before picking up Lance's sword and hitting him once more on the head, this time knocking him out. He stood and lifted Lance from the ground, throwing him over his shoulder. He picked up the sword in his other hand and walked Lance out of the castle and past the fence line, where he dropped him to the ground. Fox planted the sword into the grass in front of him, with the helmet resting on the hilt, and returned to his castle, leaving Lance unconscious on the side of the road.

chapter

NINETEEN

Lance tried to sit upright in the bed but fell to the floor as his head spun. He rolled over onto his back after landing on all fours and lay back down on the cold concrete floor. The encounter with Fox was all a blur as he tried to collect his thoughts. *Was Fox really planning on planting a bomb in the school? No, that part must have been a dream*, he thought. Fox made it clear he doesn't want to do any senseless killing. Someone like that wouldn't just put a bomb onto a college campus without ensuring there would be no casualties. *Unless*, Lance thought as a wave of nausea joined his dizziness, *that's why he spared me last night*. Lance rolled back to his side to grab the trashcan under the table, pulling it in closely to vomit into it before lying back down, falling asleep with the burden of having the lives of countless students on his shoulders, with the outcome resting on his ability to best Fox, something he had just failed miserably to do.

"Lance."

He heard a muffled voice calling as he felt himself being shaken.

"Lance, are you okay?"

More shaking. Lance tried to ignore it and continue resting, closing his eyes tighter.

"Lance!" a new voice roared, causing him to jolt awake and look around.

"Good, you're up," Jason said, standing from his crouch and walking to his station, leaving Taylor to take care of Lance.

"Where have you been?" Lance groaned as he propped himself up on one arm.

"We had to go help Hailey and Gwen clean up. We told them we would help. Don't worry, we covered for you. Now, how did you end up on the floor?"

"I tried to sit up, and I failed," Lance answered, shaking his head. "Miserably," he added after a pause.

"Jason, help me get him back up on the bed."

Jason jogged back over and helped Taylor lift him.

"We need to figure out our next move."

"Jason, did you not see me last night? I'm sure Taylor still has Fox's highlight reel on his computer if you need to rewatch it." Lance threw an arm toward the computer, but the sudden movement made him nauseous again. He put his arm back on the bed to steady himself. "There is no next move. I stand no chance against him. Our only move is to give Hailey and the campus police notice that something is going down at the chemistry building next week and hope they trust the White Knight. That's all we have."

"You're being overdramatic. It wasn't that bad. You didn't know he would be that good, and you went in underestimating him. Now that you know what to expect, you'll have a better shot at beating him."

"It's not that, Jason. I didn't lose because I underestimated him; I lost because he was better than me. Much better. I've spent ten years practicing fencing. He's spent thirty practicing swordsmanship. I don't have a prayer of defeating him." Lance shifted his weight and slowly stood. "I'll leave you two to sort out what the letter to Hailey and the police should say, and I'll deliver it later. I'm going for a walk."

Lance hobbled out the door and crossed the street to campus. He passed students as he headed toward the library, and an overwhelming dread overcame him. *How could I think I could stop Fox? The police won't listen to me. They can't stand the White Knight. And no matter how much Hailey trusts the White Knight, she can't use the paper to tell students not to go to class.* Lance couldn't think of a single thing he could do to save the students. He was going to fail.

"Lance!"

He heard someone call his name as he walked past the student union and turned to see Ashley jogging toward him.

"Hey Ashley, how are you?"

"I'm doing great, but you don't look too well. Are you okay?"

"Yeah, I'm fine. Jason and I were wrestling around last night, and he got the better of me."

"I'll say," she said, looking him up and down before giving him a skeptical look. "Hard to believe that you're that hurt after just wrestling with your roommate."

"Yeah, well, I'm not the toughest. I don't mean to be rude, but I just woke up not too long ago and was going to get lunch."

"I haven't eaten yet either. I'll go with you!" she said, grinning.

"Great," Lance muttered. "Where would you like to eat?" he asked as they made their way into the union.

"Well, it's the weekend, so most of the real restaurants are closed in the union, so I think I'll get something from the burger shop."

"I think that's what I'm getting too," he answered, holding the door open for her.

"Are you sure you're okay?" Ashley asked again after they had sat at a corner table with their food.

"Just as okay as the last time you asked. Just sore," Lance answered, picking up his burger.

"That's not what I meant," she said, throwing hair out of her face, "I know I don't know you that well, but you're also really bad at hiding your feelings. Like, exceptionally bad. Something is bothering you. You look stressed."

"Well, I graduate in four weeks, and I have no idea what I'm going to be doing in five weeks. So, yeah, that's a little stressful."

"Are you sure it's not deeper? Because while that's definitely something to stress about, you look like there is something life and death weighing on you."

"What's your major?"

"Psychology."

"Figures," he said, taking a bite of his burger. "Trust me," he continued after chewing, "I'm fine. What about you? What do you have coming up?"

"Other than my finals, all I have left is one paper and a chemistry test a week from Monday."

Lance's heart dropped, and he tuned her out as he thought. Chemistry professors almost always scheduled their exams for the same day. If there were tests that day, people would be showing up, no matter what he did. And worse, he knew people in those classes. He was sitting across from one.

"You know," he began as he got to his feet, "you were right earlier. I haven't been feeling well and I'm thinking this burger wasn't a great decision. I'm going to head back home. Good luck with your paper and test." He bumped into a table backing away, leaving her sitting there in stunned silence with her mouth open halfway through a sentence.

Walking into the base, he found Jason working on his equipment and Taylor at the computer, breaking down Fox's fighting.

"We have a problem," he told them.

"On a scale of one to a billionaire lunatic planting a bomb on a college campus, how big is it?" Jason asked without looking up from his table.

"There are chemistry tests all day on that Monday."

"How do you know?" Taylor asked, alarmed.

"When I went for my walk, Ashley saw me and wanted to get lunch. She's in that class. There's no way we'll be able to convince people not to show up if there are tests that day."

"So, what are we going to do about it?" Jason asked, having left his table to join them.

"There's nothing we can do about it. We're still helpless."

"That's enough, Lance. This campus, one that has been among the most violent universities for decades, hasn't had a single attack without the White Knight intervening since Gwen. We're not helpless. You're not helpless, Lance. You have to get over yourself. You've become so wrapped up in your pride over the mythology of the White Knight that you've forgotten that you're not alone. Jason is on your side. I'm on your side. You weren't alone in your failure last night. We were just as much to blame, but we recognize it and are working to be better for the next time instead of wallowing in self-pity. This is the same thing you did after Gwen was attacked."

"Maybe tone it down a bit, Taylor," Jason interjected.

"No. You want to quit, Lance? Fine, quit. But take a second and realize what that would lead to. If you quit, Fox wins. He gets his drugs, he gets his army, and then he gets whatever else he could possibly want. And that means death, lots, and lots of death. Starting with Ashley and everyone else in that building when the bomb goes off. Do you know why you didn't stand a chance of beating him last night?"

"Taylor," Jason cautioned again.

Taylor didn't falter.

Lance was staring at the ground.

"You couldn't beat him because he has nothing to do with why you're fighting. Gwen being attacked was tragic; I know that, as well as anyone, and that anger and desire for vengeance worked as perfect motivation to protect the campus from muggers. It worked fine for being a vigilante. But it's not enough to be a hero. Fox isn't a mugger. He's a billionaire, a genius, and a trained soldier. You're going to need a better reason than vengeance to beat him. You can't beat him by trying to fix what has happened in the past. You have to stop looking backward for your motivation and start looking forward for it. You blamed yourself for what happened to Gwen because you weren't there to stop it. We can't fix the past, but we can fight for a better future. The future can always be made better. If you want to be a hero, that's what you have to do this for. Are you really going to let this happen again on an even larger scale because you're more afraid of Fox than you are of all of those students dying?"

Jason leapt to his feet as Lance stood and moved toward Taylor. Taylor held his ground with a forced swallow. Lance didn't even look at Taylor, though, walking right past him to the weights to begin working out. After doing a warm-up set on the bench, he looked at where Jason and Taylor were still sitting.

"Jason, make sure my sword is charged. We're putting the chemistry building as our highest priority until Monday. If they try to bring the bomb before Monday, we'll be there. Taylor, keep an eye on the monitor and find out if Fox has any business in Franklin in the next week and a half."

Lance began lifting again, and Jason headed to work on the sword after giving Taylor a nod of approval and a slap on the shoulder. Taylor allowed himself a small smile as he sat back down at the monitor to begin looking up Fox's upcoming schedule.

TWENTY

"Lance, we have a problem," Taylor called from his station.

It was Thursday, four days before Fox would plant his bomb. They didn't have time for any new problems.

"What is it?" Lance answered, grabbing a towel to wipe the sweat from his brow as he walked from the weights to Taylor's monitor.

"One of the fraternities had a party tonight, and a large group from the party just arrived on another fraternity house's lawn."

"Is either of them Kappa Beta Kappa?"

"No, but—"

"Then, I'm not overly concerned with it right now, Taylor."

"Lance, it's the two fraternities who were involved in the fight outside of Ollie's earlier this semester. The house that is on the lawn right now is the one where the man who got jumped is a member, Phi Gamma. They had to hospitalize him after the mugging. We might be looking at some sort of a war starting between them and Delta Sigma if we don't do something."

"Just what we need right now," Lance mumbled, walking to his suit. "Is this not the kind of thing the cops can handle? This seems like something more up their alley."

"They've received multiple calls but have yet to send any officers to the scene."

"Fantastic. Of course, they haven't. Where is Jason? I could use backup for this."

"He and Hailey are on a date."

"Well, call him and get him out of it. We need him."

"Yeah, about that. I'm pretty sure it's their anniversary. There's no way I'm pulling him out of that tonight."

Lance rolled his eyes, sheathing his sword and grabbing his helmet as he walked away from the stand.

"Then at least make sure you have the police on call if things get violent. They might not show up for a small, casual fifty-person brawl, but they would certainly show up to try and catch me."

Lance closed the door behind him and made his way across campus. His new white suit made it impossible to hide, even in the darkest shadows, so he cut straight through campus at a half jog, making it to the frat house in just over five minutes. Both houses were on the lawn as he arrived and were shouting at one another. They were fifteen feet apart now and moving closer together.

At least thirty men came from the Phi Gamma party, and forty-five men came out of the Delta Sigma house, giving a total of seventy-five, Lance estimated, who were preparing to fight. Another few dozen men and women were standing in a semicircle around the lawn, watching the spectacle unfold as a low buzz of chatter and anticipation hung over them.

Why am I out here? He asked himself, standing twenty feet away from the edge of the group as he slowed to a stop. *The cops may not like me, but this is a job that is their problem a lot more than it is mine. If they don't want to show up and stop it, at least they can clean up the aftermath of it. There's no reason for me to get caught up in this when I have the Fox situation to worry about.*

He was preparing to leave so he could have Taylor contact the police when a spectator saw him and shouted out for others to look that way. Lance begrudgingly made his way through the crowd into the area between the two groups on the lawn.

"Everyone needs to go home now," he growled loud enough for everyone in attendance to hear him. "If this goes any further, all involved will have serious repercussions."

Lance's declaration was met with snickers from the crowd. A couple of the spectators came in from the side to grab Lance. Lance pushed his sword into his armor and waited for the two men to grab him. When he pushed the button, both men yelped and leapt away, clutching their electrocuted hands. Lance rushed the closer of the two, forehanding a swing into the man's knees and following up with a swing of the hilt into his head after he had fallen to the ground. His other attacker had fled into the crowd while Lance was engaging the first. The crowd had all backed up further from the lawn but remained close enough to see what was happening on it.

Lance sheathed his sword and, standing back up straight, growled again. "Everyone needs to go home now. If anything happens tonight, everyone on this lawn will pay."

This time, many men on the lawn shifted their weight and looked at one another, trying to decide if staying was worth whatever punishment the vigilante had in mind. Most of the spectators left. What had at one point been four dozen onlookers was now only a couple of handfuls. Lance waited, hoping the silence would help sober up the groups on the lawn enough for them to see it was in everyone's best interest to go home. Finally, the leader of the Phi Gamma group spoke to his men. "No one who leaves now will face any repercussions from the fraternity in any manner. Leave now, and it will be as if you had never come. I'm staying, though."

The men looked from one to another, and a half-dozen men left, leaving Phi Gamma with only twenty-four left to fight with. The leader of Delta Sigma gave his men the same offer, and two dozen of his men took him up on it, leaving Delta Sigma with thirty remaining. After they had all left, Lance stepped forward and again growled out, "This is your last chance to leave in peace. There will be consequences if this lawn isn't clear in one minute."

The two factions ignored him, immediately rushing into one another to create a brawl across the lawn. Lance leaped into the fighting, ripping men apart and slinging them off to the side, only for them to rejoin the battle once he had turned away from them. Lance was in the middle of the skirmish when he heard the sirens in the distance.

He shoved his way through the crowd of bodies to get away before the cops showed up. He had gotten too far into the fighting to easily extricate himself as the sirens grew louder. Suddenly, a red arm reached through the crowd and grabbed him. Jason pulled Lance out of the brawl, and the two took off past the house and into the nearby neighborhood. Leaping fences, they made it to the far end of campus through backyards before cutting across campus to the storage unit.

"I thought you had a date," Lance panted as they sat down inside the base.

"Hailey is going apartment hunting with Sam in the morning and, luckily for you, wanted to call it a night early."

"I would have been fine without you," Lance retorted, exhausted, leaning his head against the wall.

"Hmph."

Was all the response Jason could give as he leaned forward, resting his head in his hands.

"It looks like the police arrested thirty-five tonight after you two got away. Does that sound about right, Lance?" Taylor asked from the computer.

"I think there were closer to fifty-five left when the fighting began, but I guess a few could have left in the confusion after the fighting had started."

"Well, they're all being locked up overnight, and most of them will have to wait to go before the student courts until after they go through the real judicial process. Those were city cops that responded, not campus police."

Lance nodded, finally getting to his feet to take off his armor. Jason arose and did the same.

"When did you get a suit?" Lance asked, registering Jason's armor for the first time.

It was similar to Lance's but red. It also didn't have a sheath since he didn't carry a sword, preferring to use his spear. His suit also had a small shield built into the left arm that could fold out.

"You think you're the only one worth a suit of armor?" Jason rolled his eyes, laughing and responding, "I started working on it after I finished yours."

"I guess I should be thankful you had it tonight."

"Yes, you should," he answered as Taylor walked from the computers, having shut everything down.

Jason and Lance finished hanging up their armor. Then, they all made their way to the door.

"What do you think Hailey's headline will be in tomorrow's paper?" Lance asked as the three headed out the door to the apartment. "Maybe you'll finally get a name too, Jason."

IRONSIDE AND THE WHITE KNIGHT PREVENT FRATERNITY BRAWL

It appears that the White Knight is not the only one watching over our campus. Last night, the Phi Gamma fraternity showed up at the Delta Sigma house with a crowd as the two met on the Delta Sigma lawn. Witnesses say that many of the onlookers and even some of the fraternity members left after the White Knight arrived on the scene trying to prevent the fight. The two sides did end up in an altercation, though the White Knight had kept them apart long enough for the campus police to arrive soon after the fighting started. Thirty-five members of the fraternities were arrested, but the most intriguing event last night was who got away. The White Knight found himself in the center of the altercation as the police arrived, but witnesses say that another vigilante showed up in a red suit and pulled him out to escape before authorities arrived. Once again, thanking these campus heroes.

Hailey Hall

"What does Ironside even mean?" Jason asked across the table at breakfast as he laid the paper down and picked up his fork.

"At least she didn't call you my sidekick," Lance pointed out. "Hailey would've been so confused if you had stopped talking to her for a month without explanation."

"She would have been. I guess it could've been a lot worse, but why couldn't Ashley have been on the scene last night? Consider yourself lucky that Hailey didn't decide your name."

Lance laughed. "You're right, though. It could've been a lot worse."

TWENTY-ONE

"I see you brought a friend this time."

Fox stepped out of the back seat of his still-running car, opening an umbrella as he stood to face Lance and Jason. They stood between Fox and the chemistry building in their respective white and red suits. Taylor had seen his car pull into Franklin at a traffic light at one in the morning. Lance and Jason had rushed to get dressed and made it to the building in less than ten minutes, narrowly beating Fox. The rain was coming down hard, and the chemistry building had little lighting to begin with. Jason's suits were holding up well in the rain, but their visors were fogging from the moisture.

"No matter. This shouldn't take long. If you will excuse me, I'm just here to drop off a package, and I'll be out of your way." He stepped forward and began walking.

"You can't be serious, man," Jason scoffed, stopping Fox.

"I have been known to pull the occasional prank, but not this time. I am certainly serious. I have put a great deal of time, money, and effort into this project, and I intend to see it through, regardless of whether or not a couple of medieval cosplayers are present. Now, you can either step away and let me through, or you can meet the same fate that became your friend here just the other night."

"Step aside so that you can do what? Kill a tenth of my classmates? I don't think so."

"I sure hope not. Like I told your friend here a week ago, I don't care for senseless killings. I want this building to fall, destroying any evidence of my work here. That is all. I actually plan on having a new building built by next summer. State of the art. And I'm expecting the two of you to ensure that this building is empty on Monday when the bomb goes off."

"And why can't you set it off tonight?" Lance finally spoke up. "Why do you have to do it when it's going to be full of students?"

"Because blowing up a building in the middle of the night would bring more questions, don't you think? Why would someone just decide to blow up a building? No. Unfortunately, a terrorist attack on one of the most violent campuses in America is much more believable. And one would almost need to pull a stunt like this to cause any sort of damage to your campus with how you've been watching over it. Kudos to you on that. It really is something impressive that you've been able to do here. I even delivered the package personally because you have so frequently beaten my team here. I knew I'd have to come myself to make sure it was delivered. But"—he lowered his bag to the ground and tapped at the hilt on his hip—"it will be difficult for you to save your campus if you're lying broken and battered on a hospital bed tomorrow morning. Or in a morgue."

Fox picked his bag back up and walked forward again as Jason lowered into a stance with his spear tucked under his arm, pointing out toward Fox while Lance drew his sword. Fox sighed and drew his own sword, placing the bag back on the ground and setting the umbrella down with it, crouching into a fighting stance as he did so. Lance and Jason shuffled apart from one another to force Fox to fight in two directions. The three remained in a fighting stance as they studied one another as the rain fell harder. Lightning cracked behind the chemistry building, and Jason used the opportunity to lunge at Fox. Fox quickly deflected before turning to block a jab by Lance. Lance and Jason circled him, his smirk gone. In its place was the stern concentration of a battle-hardened soldier and an expert of his craft. Lance feinted left as Jason lunged once more. Fox parried Jason's lunge while sidestepping another one of Lance's jabs. Both stumbled past Fox, who tripped up Jason as he passed by, sending him to the ground and then engaging Lance.

Lance blocked Fox's first strike and then his second, but Fox was quickly pushing Lance back. He was forced to hop to avoid a slash at his legs. Lance was still in the air when he heard the thud that knocked the breath out of him. Fox had been pushing him back toward the car where he would have nowhere else to go, and his momentum slammed him into the car while he was still airborne. Lance collapsed on the ground against the car at Fox's feet.

"I tried to avoid this." Fox placed the tip of his sword on Lance's exposed throat, kicking Lance's sword out of his hand. "I told you what I was going to do and when I would do it. All you needed to do was make sure that this building was empty Monday when the bomb went off. I would have completed my work here on your campus, and your campus would be just as safe as it had been before, with not a single person perishing in the explosion. But the safety of your classmates wasn't enough for you, was it? No, for some reason, you decided that you were going to pick a fight with me. A fight that you never had a prayer of winning. It's sad, really. I still believe you could've helped me do great things to change this world. But you've made your choice, and with choices come consequences." He gave a sad smile, drawing back his sword.

Lance closed his eyes as the sword was drawn back, his whole body becoming tense. A scream pierced the night as Jason's spear dove into Fox's shoulder. A look of terror followed the scream as Fox fell to one knee.

Lance leapt to his feet with his sword, picking it back up from where Fox had kicked it. Fox clenched his jaw and yanked the spear from his back. The spear's head glowed bright in the rainy night sky, light leaping from it with every drop to land upon the electrified head. Fox rocked from side to side, his sword drawn as he tried to regain his balance. His smirk was once again gone, having been replaced by a grimace. Fox snarled, his sword facing Lance as he shuffled in Jason's direction when suddenly he froze. A siren broke through the night air. Fox stared from Lance to Jason and back to Lance as he sheathed his sword as the sirens became louder. He grabbed the bag with the bomb and his umbrella before he hobbled back to his car, taking off as the flashing lights were now visible only a block away.

Jason chased after Fox as he ran for his car until Lance grabbed him, pulling him into the alley's shadows with him. They escaped into the strip between two buildings just as the lights pulled up to the front. Jason was already sprinting up the fire escape when Lance turned away from the lights. He quickly followed Jason up the escape and back to the base, using the roofs and fire escapes the buildings provided.

"What was that?" Jason bellowed as he followed Lance into the storage unit.

"You are going to have to be more specific. A lot just happened," Lance answered, taking off his helmet and hanging it on the hook inside of his case.

"Okay. What were you thinking, letting that madman get away?" Jason took his own helmet off and threw it against the wall. "We had him! You think he won't plant the bomb again? He will. And next time, he won't give you an advanced warning for you to save people. We're in a worse position now than we were an hour ago."

"What did you want me to do? You weren't going to chase him down when he was driving. The cops would've shown up, caught us both, and we would've been done. And he would still have the bomb. This way, we live to fight another day."

"I wanted you to do something when you had the chance. After I caught him in the shoulder, he froze, paralyzed as the electricity coursed through his body. And you did nothing."

"You wanted me to kill him?"

"I don't know! Maybe! He plans on killing tens or hundreds of thousands of people. Would killing him to prevent that from happening really be that bad? Would that not be justified?"

"The just outcome is not always the same as the right one. I've never killed anyone before, so, yeah, I hesitated in my first time in that position. I'm not ready to cross that line into being an executioner. But by all means, be my guest to kill the bad guy next time."

"Fine, Gandhi, but you're gambling with people's lives. This man will kill people you know, people you care about, whether he knows who you really are or not. And he'll start by getting a building named after him on this campus after he blows one up that's filled with students." Jason stormed away to his workstation to remove his soaking suit, picking up his helmet on his way.

Lance walked to the suit mount and undressed. He took off his breastplate and arm guards and hung them up. He removed his second layer of armor and left it to the side to dry out. After removing his padded gloves, he sat on the bench and put his head in his hands. *Did I make the wrong decision? Am I really capable of taking a man's life? Even if it were to save countless others? No. Jason might be right that it would be justified, but that isn't a line I'm willing to cross. Not yet, and maybe not ever. We'll have to find another way.*

A hand rested on his shoulder. He looked up to see Taylor, who had patiently waited for tempers to cool before approaching.

"Do you have any injuries I need to take care of?"

"No. Just some bruises. Thanks."

"Jason's right. You would have been justified in killing him when you had a chance. But right and wrong isn't always as black and white as justice is. It may be a little right to kill him, but more right to spare him. That's something only the person faced with that choice can decide. If you think you did the right thing, then I think so, too. I have faith in your judgment. Jason does, too. He'll come around. He's as stressed about this as you are. He just shows it differently. You need to talk to him. You two can't be on opposite sides. Not right now. You need each other to protect the campus." Taylor patted his back and rose up to walk back to his monitor to scan the video feeds. Lance walked to Jason.

"We need to be on the same page, Lance. We can't fight together with different goals in mind."

"Our goals are the same. It's the means we plan on using to get there that aren't. Killing isn't a step I'm willing to take right now. If you think it's necessary, then that's your prerogative."

"You didn't have to kill him. He was paralyzed in shock. You could have knocked him down, knocked him out, done something else. You had options."

"I get that, but two seconds earlier, I thought I was dead. I didn't react in time, but in that moment, I was already in a life-or-death state. Those were the only things in my head. Kill him or let him live. And I couldn't make that call." Jason nodded but didn't respond. "How do we keep him from blowing up the building?"

"Well, we won't be able to stop him from planting it without knowing when he plans on doing so. We will need Taylor to monitor the campus for different signs that could be coming from a bomb, and then we'll have to disarm it."

"Do you think you could do that?"

Jason looked up to Lance as a smile broke out across his face. "Of course I can."

chapter

TWENTY-TWO

"Lance, Taylor, come on," Jason begged as he stood in the base doorway, his backpack on his shoulders. "It's just a couple hours, and it's still the middle of the day. Nothing is going to happen requiring the White Knight's services."

"We have to figure this out, Jason," Taylor answered from the computer, not even turning toward Jason.

"Not sure if you already forgot about what happened last night, but we're at a huge disadvantage even with the two of us. He could have killed me if he wanted to twice now. We have to stop him before Monday, and we have no idea how. This is more important than studying."

"Look, we promised Gwen and Hailey we would meet them at the union at two. It's just for a little bit. It would do us all good to get out of here anyway. See the sun for once. Lately, it feels like the only time we're not in the base is when we're stopping something. This stuff is important, but we're dangerously close to letting this be the only part of our lives."

"If we don't figure it out, there are going to be a lot of people, maybe even including us, who lose their lives entirely," Lance answered him.

"That's true. But you're not actually figuring anything out right now. Neither of you are. Are you? No? That's what I thought. You're just sitting here being anxious and stressing yourself out and making the odds of you being able to stop him smaller because you're exhausting yourself. We have to stop Fox, yes, but right now, the ball is in his court. We can't do anything until he makes his next move. So please, take a break. Come with me to see Hailey and Gwen."

"He's got a point, Lance. We have been in here too much lately. And as much as I want to be able to figure out the puzzle of the exact thing to do to stop Fox, there really isn't anything we can do right now. I think we should go," Taylor responded, grabbing his messenger bag, and slinging it over his shoulder.

"Then go with him. I'm staying." Lance picked up the notepad he had been writing and then crossing things out in.

"Lance," Jason said before Lance had even finished talking. "For the first time in weeks, we can all spend time together, just the five of us. You can spend time with Gwen for the first time in weeks. If something does happen to you Monday, wouldn't you want to have seen her before then?"

Lance set his notebook down and leaned back against the wall, closing his eyes.

"Two hours. Max. Then we all come back and focus. Agreed?"

"Done," Jason answered, beaming.

Lance sighed, hopped off the medical bed, and grabbed his backpack from the floor. Jason left the door open behind him as Taylor and Lance walked across the unit to catch up to him, Lance closing it behind him on the way out. It was a nice spring day, so they walked to the union even though it was on the other side of campus.

The courtyard was full of students studying for upcoming finals. Every outdoor table was occupied, and a handful of groups were scattered around, sitting on the grass and working under trees. There were two hammocks hung up between a couple of trees, and Lance felt a pang of guilt as he saw Ashley reading a book in one with a redheaded girl in the other. A shiver ran down his spine, but he shook it off and opened the door to the union for the other two.

The inside of the union was as crowded as the courtyard was. A steady buzz filled the room as groups at each table thought out loud while they crammed for tests. The three stood at the entrance, looking around to see if they could spot the girls in the crowded room.

Jason lightly slapped Lance's chest and pointed across the room where Hailey and Gwen were waving their arms in the air. Lance tapped Taylor and waved at him to follow them. They navigated through the crowds of students looking for a seat at a table.

"We were starting to think you all had ditched us," Hailey said as the three of them sat in the booth.

Lance and Taylor joined Gwen on one side while Jason sat beside Hailey.

"We just lost track of time." Jason smiled back at her.

"What were you doing?" Gwen asked, turning to Lance and Taylor.

"Uh . . . we were . . . um . . ." Taylor stammered as Hailey and Gwen watched him.

"We had taken a nap." Lance stepped in to answer. "We were up late studying last night and didn't get much sleep, so we thought we would get in a power nap before coming over here. Jason was the only one to wake up to his alarm, and it took him time to wake us up. You know how deep Taylor sleeps. He's still trying to wake up."

"You always were tough to wake up," Gwen laughed as Taylor let out a deep breath.

Lance and Jason caught each other's eye before Jason broke the brief silence.

"Where's Sam at today?" he asked Hailey.

"He had some stuff he was having to take care of up in Duncan. He should be back tomorrow. What are you two studying?" she asked Lance and Taylor.

"I'm still trying to figure out some of these conjugations for Spanish," Lance answered.

"Neurobiology," Taylor answered. "This class will be the death of me."

"Do you mind switching me places, Taylor?" Gwen asked, looking down the booth. "It would help if I was closer to Hailey and Jason since we're all studying for the same history class."

"Yeah, that's fine," Taylor answered, scooting out of the booth so that Lance and Gwen could let him back in. "It will be easier to study in the corner of the booth anyway. I won't have people brushing by me all the time."

As they reorganized themselves in the booth, a nearby group leered at them as they walked off.

"You three getting up made them think we were leaving," Jason laughed as Taylor pulled out his textbook, and Lance and Gwen turned to look at the group walking away.

"Oh, now I feel bad," Gwen sighed.

"We didn't do anything wrong, Gwen," Lance assured her. "They'll find another table."

"I guess."

"Don't feel bad," Hailey told her. "I interviewed one of those guys, and he was a jerk to me the whole time.

I hope they aren't able to find a table, they can't study, and they fail their tests."

"Dang, Hall, bringing out the big guns," Lance laughed.

"I just can't stand guys like him. He talked to me like I was a child who didn't know anything."

"I told her she had to push a door that she tried pulling on the night that interview happened, and we spent the rest of the night getting some good conflict resolution practice in," Jason added.

"Well, you're in luck, Hall. With how crazy it is in here today, there's a good chance they won't find a place to study."

"Speaking of which," Gwen interjected, "we should probably get started ourselves."

Jason and Lance grudgingly pulled out their books to study. Hailey and Gwen had theirs out when they had arrived, and Taylor had ignored the last few minutes of conversation after he had started studying.

Lance joined Taylor in solo studying while the other three practiced together using flash cards for their test. Occasionally, he would ask Gwen for help with his Spanish, and she would always take the time to help him while Hailey and Jason continued studying without her.

"Lance, if you put 'sabo' on your test instead of 'se,' your professor will not only fail you, they're going to see to it that you're expelled. There is no bigger sin in Spanish class than that."

"But, on every other verb, you drop the—er and add an O to make it first person present. How are you getting 'se' from saber?"

"How did you make it to Spanish two still making that mistake, Locke?"

"You and Gwen."

"It's just one of the irregular verbs," Gwen laughed. "You just have to remember that one is special."

Lance shook his head, but he was smiling. Jason was right. Even with how wrapped up he had been in being the White Knight, he had missed the five of them spending time together, even if it was to study. Hearing Gwen's laugh had him kicking himself for pushing her away and letting that distance between them linger and fester. They hadn't had a chance to talk one-on-one since they reconciled at Taylor's party, and he wasn't sure exactly where they stood. It was different than before they stopped talking and definitely different than before December, but he was unable to quite figure out how differently she felt now. How much her trust had been broken. There was definitely a lot of work to be done to earn back that trust, but for now, getting to hear her laugh again was a win.

As they continued studying, the union cleared out as the students left for dinner breaks away from their study space. Lance's two hours had turned into four, and while he didn't want this time with Gwen and Hailey to end, he was anxious to get back to the base.

"We should probably wrap it up here pretty soon," Lance announced, pushing his book away from him.

"I was thinking the same thing," Hailey said, closing her book as well. "Let's go get some dinner."

"Oh. We, um, actually were planning to take care of some stuff tonight. Maybe another time?" Lance responded.

"What kind of stuff?" Gwen asked.

"We were just going to try and get a gym session in," Jason cut in. "Physical exercise is supposed to help you focus more, so we were going to go to the Rec to focus on something else for a bit."

"I mean, you still have to eat, though, right? Just go after!" Hailey pointed out.

"That's a good point," Taylor answered, with Jason and Lance turning to him and raising their eyebrows. "Let's go grab a bite, and then we can head to the Rec after that. Sound good?"

"Sounds great," Hailey answered.

"Ollie's?" Gwen asked.

"Yeah, that sounds great," Taylor answered, putting his textbook away.

Lance widened his eyes at Jason, who shrugged and packed away his index cards and textbook. Lance sighed and put his stuff in his bag, too.

"What was that about?" he asked Taylor after they said goodbye to Hailey and Gwen outside Ollie's and walked back to the storage unit.

"There wasn't a non-suspicious way to tell them we couldn't get dinner with them, so I told them we could instead of waiting for one of you two to tip them off."

Lance opened his mouth to argue, but Jason stopped him with a hand on his shoulder. "You know he's right. They weren't going to buy us having to leave somewhere. It was the right call."

"Fine," Lance sighed. "But can we please go back to the base and focus now? We only have about thirty-six hours to figure out what Fox is going to do on Monday and how to stop him."

"We're going to stop him, Lance," Taylor answered as they walked away. "Let's go figure out how."

chapter

TWENTY-THREE

"None of these ideas are going to stop him," Jason said. He leaned forward in his chair, putting his head in his hands and letting out a groan as he did so.

They had spent the past five hours brainstorming ways to stop Fox from getting the bomb in place and setting it off on Monday. They had a whiteboard set up that they had taken turns writing and drawing on, a corkboard with strings connecting people and places to ideas, and a trash can full of crumpled-up pieces of paper. What they still didn't have was a plan.

"That's not helpful, Jason," Taylor chided him.

"No," Lance said, shaking his head, "but it's true. We're no closer to stopping him now than we were this morning. He's smarter than us, more skilled than us, has access to more resources than we do, and has been planning this a lot longer than we have."

"Not to mention he has the campus and civil authorities on his side, and the ball is in his court. He gets to act while we're forced to react."

"That, too."

"Guys," Taylor said, "we can figure this out. There's three of us and only one of him—"

"Actually, he has a fraternity, a professor, some bodyguards, and who knows how many other people working on this."

"Still not helpful, Jason," Taylor continued as Jason shrugged. "He's not going to have all those people strategizing with him. He won't be able to have all those people on hand when he's planting the bomb. We have him outnumbered where it matters. We just have to come up with a plan."

"Do we, though?" Lance asked, leaning forward in his chair.

"Yes, why are both of you being so negative? Didn't we say this whole thing was about light and hope now? Where'd that attitude go?"

"No, no, no," Lance shook his head, standing. "Maybe we've been going about this the wrong way. Jason is right. The ball is in his court, and there's not a whole lot we can do without knowing his plan. We just have to be prepared to react. That's all we can do. We can't clear the building beforehand, so we just have to be prepared to move at any time on Monday. What are your schedules like?"

"I've got a history test with Hailey and Gwen, but other than that, I can be here."

"I don't have anything that day. It's a study day in my classes. I can be here all day watching the monitors," Taylor answered.

"And I have a couple of final reviews, but I can keep my phone on the table during those and leave if I need to. We just have to all be ready to move at any time."

"I don't know. I think I'd still feel more comfortable with a plan."

"I would too, Taylor, but I'm starting to think that's not an option. All we're doing is killing ourselves and burning out without getting anywhere. We need to be sharp on Monday to react and what we've been doing is just going to tire us out."

"Lance is right. We should call it a night and spend tomorrow doing whatever we each need to do to be fresh on Monday. We're just going to have to do some improv."

"I still don't like this plan."

"Well, technically, it's not a plan, so that's fine," Jason laughed as he got out of his chair.

"You just got to have a little hope, Taylor." Lance smiled and offered his hand to help him stand. "That's what we're all about, right?"

The three returned to their apartment a little before one am, and each retired to their rooms to rest. Even after his earlier argument to be prepared to react, Lance was still unsure about the wisdom of that course. He just didn't see another option. He tossed and turned, trying to get comfortable, but, seemingly, no matter what he did, it felt like he was lying on a knot.

An hour passed, then two, with Lance fading in and out of sleep. He finally fell asleep for longer than twenty minutes straight, a little after three in the morning, but not even three more hours passed before he was up again.

The sun had yet to rise, but the pre-dawn sky had begun to lighten as he sat up on the edge of the bed. He grabbed his hoodie from his desk chair as he walked across the room. He threw that on over his T-shirt, pulled on his jeans, and laced his tennis shoes. He hurriedly brushed his teeth and washed his face before silently walking through the apartment and out the door, heading to the stairwell.

The green sky was beginning its transition to yellow as he walked away from the apartment complex and down the sidewalk. His mind raced as he tried to push away the anxiety of what awaited him tomorrow.

The cool morning air helped dull his anxiety in part, but he needed to do something to get his mind off of what was coming.

Ten minutes after he started his walk from the apartment, he came to a stop on the sidewalk. He took a deep breath, letting his shoulders lift as he inhaled and then fall as he exhaled before jogging up to the door. He knocked three times and stepped back, away from the door.

He waited as twenty seconds passed, then thirty. He knocked again. Another thirty seconds passed, and he started to walk back to the sidewalk when he heard the click of the locks.

Gwen opened the door, rubbing at her eyes as the morning sunlight greeted her through the storm door. Her sandy hair was in two braids that fell one on each side of her face, and she wore a robe over a T-shirt and pajama pants.

"Lance?" she yawned as she spoke through the screen door. "What are you doing here? It's not even seven o'clock yet."

"I thought we could go get Sunday morning breakfast like we used to. We haven't had much time to talk lately, and with our last semester wrapping up, I thought it would be nice to bring back that tradition one last time."

"You could have given me more notice," she yawned again.

"I know. I should have. I didn't really plan it. I just wanted to see you, and I thought getting breakfast again might be nice."

"It would be nice." She smiled at him through the door before opening it and stepping to the side. "Come sit in the living room while I get dressed. It shouldn't take too long."

He smiled back at her, walked in, and sat on the couch. Ten minutes later, she came back out in her leggings and an oversized sweatshirt, her braids replaced by a hat and ponytail.

"Where to?" she asked, locking the door behind her as she joined Lance to walk down the steps in front of her house.

"Fozzie's, of course. I told you this is a last hurrah for old times' sake. There's nowhere else we could go." Lance lightly elbowed her as they walked together down the sidewalk away from campus.

Gwen smiled but didn't respond, and the two walked in silence. They had stopped the bleeding at Taylor's party, but the relational wounds hadn't healed yet. In the past, they had spent hours together in comfortable silence, but after the past few months, this silence was anything but comfortable. Still, it persisted.

Lance opened the door for her as they reached Fozzie's, and they took their usual booth against the far window.

"Long time no see," the middle-aged waitress greeted as she walked up. "Nice to have you two back."

"It's good to be back," Gwen answered, smiling up at the waitress first and then at Lance.

"I'll be back for your orders in just a minute," she said as she filled up their mugs with coffee and left two glasses of water on the table.

Lance took a sip and made a face. "Coffee's just as bad as it used to be."

"You wanted it to be like old times," Gwen laughed as she poured creamers and sugar into hers to make it drinkable.

"I would've been okay with that change." He smiled at her and waited for her to pass the creamer to him. "At least it's cheap."

"What can I get started for you?" the waitress asked as she returned with a notepad.

"I'll do the breakfast sampler," Lance answered.

"How do you want your eggs?"

"Scrambled."

"Meat?"

"Bacon."

"Gotcha. And for you?"

"I'll do the French toast with a side of oatmeal," Gwen said with a smile as she handed her menu over.

"You got it. Give us a few minutes, and we'll have that out."

"Thanks."

Lance and Gwen laughed as they said it at the same time.

"Just like old times."

"Like old times," Gwen agreed before the table fell into the silence again.

After thirty seconds of them looking around the diner, Lance said, "We should keep this tradition when we get to Duncan."

"I'd like that." Gwen smiled across the table at him. She lifted her mug up to take a sip, and it was her turn to make a face. "All that creamer and it still tastes awful."

"That's what gives this place character. We can try and find a spot with better coffee to become regulars at in Duncan."

"Better coffee is a must," Gwen laughed, setting her mug back down and taking a drink of her water instead. A few beats passed before she spoke again. "You seem better now, Lance."

"What do you mean?"

"When we stopped talking, you seemed distant, broken almost. You looked beaten up. You acted beaten up. But you seem better now."

"I am. I still feel like I have the weight of the world coming down on me," he chuckled and shook his head, "but I don't know. I feel like I've learned to manage it better. I'm still anxious about everything, but I feel less overwhelmed. I would have gotten there sooner if I hadn't pushed you away." She looked down at her coffee as he said that. He put his hand on hers. "I've gotten better the past month or so, but I wasn't good again until we were good again. I wish I hadn't had to wait for you to stop talking to me to get better, but it was the wake-up call I needed. Because I can't do this without you, Gwen."

She looked up from the table and smiled at him, though he could see sadness in her eyes.

"What is it?" he asked.

"I just have a lot of conflicting feelings. I'm thankful you're doing better, and I'm glad we're spending time together again, but the hurt of the past few months is still lingering, and it puts a bittersweet taste on all of this."

"I understand."

She shook her head. "It's hard because I'm not sure what our relationship was before all this, what it is now, or even what I want it to be. We've been closer than friends for a while now, but that never turned into anything more, no matter how much I hoped it would at times. And now, are we trying to work back to that place? Are we trying to just become friends again? Are we trying to be more than that? I don't know where we're at, and I'm not sure what answer I'm hoping for from you, but I need to know what you're feeling, Lance. We've gone through too much just to have this floating out there unresolved."

Lance took a deep breath and gulped as she finished talking. She stared across the table at him, looking him in the eyes as she waited for his response. He opened his mouth to respond but was cut off as the waitress returned.

"Order up," she said, laughing to herself as she sat the plates down in front of them. "Here's your checks. Just take them to the front when you're done."

"Thank you," Gwen responded with a smile.

"Uh, yeah, thanks," Lance added as she walked away. He took another deep breath and looked back at Gwen to find she was staring at him again, waiting for his answer.

"Gwen, I—" He took another deep breath and looked down at the table to compose himself. "Gwen," he laughed and looked into her eyes, "if I knew the answer, I would tell you right now. I swear I would. I've spent so long asking myself that same question. It's been years. I love you, Gwen, and I always have. I've had plenty of times where I wanted this to be more than it was, too. But I've always stopped myself from pursuing that because I could never risk losing your friendship. I'm sure that being in a relationship with you would be all I've hoped it could be, but I also know that were that not to work out, the emptiness I would feel losing you from my life would be too much to bear. These past few weeks separated from you have only reinforced for me how much I need you in my life. So, I don't really know exactly what my feelings are right now, and that's complicated all the more by knowing that your feelings are also complicated right now."

"Is it okay for me to not know right now? I promise to be honest and straightforward with you about my feelings and intentions. I want to be able to answer your question, but I still need to unravel all of my own feelings and emotions and baggage to do that. Right now, I just want to focus on earning back your trust and making up for lost time in our friendship because I was acting a fool these last few months. Is that fair?"

"You promise to tell me when you figure out what you feel?"

"Pinky promise."

"Then yeah, that's fair. This is already the most honest conversation we've had about this topic. It feels . . ." She stared out the window. "Good. I think. Yeah. It's a weird good, but it's good."

"I agree," Lance answered as he took a bite of eggs. "I'm just glad we're back."

"Me, too." She smiled at him as she cut into her French toast, and that comfortable silence that had eluded them all day surrounded them once again as they ate.

It was almost eleven by the time they made it back to Gwen's house. Their conversation had opened the floodgates that they had constructed over the past few months, and they talked about everything they had been missing in each other's lives, well, almost everything, as Lance still kept his alter ego a secret from her.

They finally had to return so Gwen could make it to a study group lunch for her history test the next day.

"I'll text you later," Lance promised as he backed down the stairs off her porch.

"I'd like that. It was good to just be with you again, Lance."

"I promise it won't be as long before we do it again."

"I'm going to hold you to that." Gwen smiled as she waved before closing the door.

Lance turned back toward the apartment complex once he made it back to the sidewalk, unable to resist doing a little skip as he left the house.

Taylor jumped as Lance opened the door to the apartment.

"We thought you were in bed asleep this whole time," Taylor said as he repositioned himself on the couch.

"Where've you been?" Jason asked, pulling his head out of the fridge as Lance closed the door behind.

"Couldn't sleep." Lance shrugged. "I went to breakfast with Gwen at Fozzie's. I thought about what Jason said about going into tomorrow without having really talked to her. The group hangout was fun, but I needed to see her one-on-one for a bit."

"Good to hear. We need you firing on all cylinders tomorrow," Jason answered as he put two slices of bread on his plate to make his sandwich.

"I will be. I'm going to take a nap to try and recoup some of my lost sleep from last night."

"Don't sleep too long," Taylor warned. "It's important for you to get a full night's sleep tonight to be ready for tomorrow."

"After this morning, I've never felt more ready for tomorrow. Fox hasn't gotten our best yet. Tomorrow, he's going to find out what that looks like."

TWENTY-FOUR

He's here.

All it took was a two-word text from Taylor for Lance to bolt out of his lecture. Slinging his bag over his shoulder and grabbing his notebook, he left his pen on the desk as everyone stared at him while he shuffled to the end of the row so he could head straight for the storage unit. They were two-thirds through the final review, but it didn't matter now. He passed a group of girls walking into the chemistry building and took off in a sprint as people moved out of his way while giving him dirty looks. He didn't have the luxury of walking. Not right now.

"Where is he?" Lance asked, slinging the door open.

"He's talking with the president. He went in fifteen minutes ago."

Lance took his base layer off of the rack and dressed. "Does he have the bomb?"

"I'm not sure. He doesn't have it with him, but it could be in the car. I only found him because the security camera outside the president's office picked him up coming in."

"Have you gotten a hold of Jason?"

"No. His phone's off. I think he has a history test with Gwen and Hailey."

"Where is their test?"

"I believe it's in Mulder. Why?"

"Because that's right next to the chemistry building. His phone shouldn't be off. He knows that today is the day Fox is making his move. Keep trying to get in contact with him and make sure the girls are far away from the building in case something happens."

"I'll try."

Lance finished putting on his armor and attached his sword to his belt. He grabbed his helmet and walked toward the door.

"What do you think you're doing?"

"I'm going to stop Fox."

"You're going to walk across campus in your armor, with a sword around your waist? Then you're going to walk into the chemistry building to fight a billionaire who may or may not have a bomb? That's the plan?"

"What are my other options right now, Taylor?" he asked; his voice was harsher than Taylor deserved, but he was feeling the stress of the situation too strongly at the moment to care.

"At the very least, wait until Fox leaves the president's office so you don't show up at the chemistry building before he even gets there. The campus police will have you arrested before he arrives, and he'll be able to plant the bomb unbothered."

Lance paced next to the door, waiting for Taylor to give him a signal. He was feeling the heat of the suit from his pacing. It was mid-April, and they had just had their first heat wave of the season. It had come later in the year than was usual, but it made up for the delay with extra heat. Three of the last four days had been in the mid-nineties.

"He's on the move!" Taylor hollered from his computer, and Lance rushed over to watch the monitor. "His car just picked him up. It looks like they're headed to the chemistry building. I'll keep you updated as you move."

Lance sprinted for the door and took off across the road. Horns blared, and brakes screeched as he rushed through the busy street. Lance could see Fox stepping out of his car, briefcase in hand. He was still a hundred yards away as Fox walked up the steps to the building. Students stopped on their way across campus to take photos and videos of Lance in his suit as he made his way up the steps. Right before he could reach the door, though, it flew open as Matthew Fox hurried out. The sight of Lance seemed to startle him, but he quickly shook it off, running up and grabbing him by the shoulders.

"I have just been notified that a bomb threat has just been called in!" Fox screamed for everyone to hear him. "Someone is in the basement lab with an armed bomb. You have to do something. I'll try and get as many out of the building as I can, but you have to go and stop the bomb."

He released his shoulders and stepped back, allowing Lance to make it to the door. Panic set in among all the students who heard his announcement. In a voice low enough that only Lance could hear him, he added, "You don't have much time. I suggest you hurry. I don't want to see anyone die any more than you do."

Lance watched as Fox hurried off into the building and banged on classroom doors, telling students to leave. Lance stepped in his direction to go after him before Taylor's voice came over his headset.

"You don't have time for Fox. He was telling the truth. Campus police just posted an alert saying they had a bomb threat in the chemistry building. You need to get to that lab ASAP."

Lance turned and sprinted for the stairwell, telling everyone he passed to get people out of the building.

"Set off the fire alarm so people will know to get out," Lance barked into the headset as he yanked open the stairwell door, the fire alarm blaring out immediately.

He took the stairs three at a time, going down, and found the lab door across from the stairwell was locked. He stepped back and kicked the door. Nothing happened. The steel door wasn't budging as he kicked at it again.

"How do I get in?" he growled into his headset as the fire alarm blared around him.

He heard keys being rapidly hit, and then Taylor's voice returned.

"There should be a vent right above you. It leads into the lab. Can you get up to it?"

Lance looked around for something to stand on. There was nothing in the hallway. He ran into the nearest classroom, pulled a chair out of it, and placed it under the vent. He climbed onto the chair and reached for the vent, but it wouldn't budge either.

"Is there a plan C?" he asked Taylor.

"We don't have time for a plan C. Pry it open with your sword."

Lance unsheathed his sword, fitted it between the vent and ceiling, and pulled down. The vent wiggled but stayed in place. He tried again, pulling harder, but to no avail. The third time he pulled, he fell off his chair. Still grasping the sword, his fall helped to free the vent from the ceiling. He rolled onto his back and reached for his ankle, letting out a groan as it twisted underneath his weight from his fall.

"Lance, are you okay?" Taylor asked as Lance lay on his back.

"Fine," Lance grunted. "The vent is open."

He pulled himself to his feet before climbing back onto the chair. He sheathed his sword and pulled himself up into the vent. He barely had room to wiggle his shoulders as he crawled through the shaft. He came to the first opening thirty seconds and twenty-five feet later.

"Is this the lab?" he panted.

"Yes. Hurry," was all Taylor said.

Lance pulled his sword out, only able to pull it inches at a time, which took him another ten seconds he didn't have, and slammed the hilt of the sword into the opening once he finally got it in front of him. The vent gave way on the third attempt, and Lance tumbled down into the lab, landing on a table before falling to the ground. Lance tried to hurry to his feet, only to fall back down. Jason's suit provided a measure of protection from the fall, but he was still shaken. He had reaggravated his ankle, and the fall had made him lightheaded.

He got to his feet again, slowly this time, and surveyed his surroundings. There was nothing. *No bomb, no bomber, nothing. I'm in the wrong lab,* he thought to himself. *Fox wanted me to find the bomb. Why would he lock the door? It must be in one of the smaller labs.*

Lance picked up his sword from where it had fallen and rushed back to the door leading back to the hall when he heard a muffled yell and crash. Turning back around, Lance saw nothing where the sound came from. He walked back across the lab and found hinges coming out of a chalkboard on the side of the room. Upon closer inspection, Lance saw a groove in the board. He grabbed the groove and pulled, causing a student, bound and gagged, to fall out of the closet. He quickly took off the gag covering the student's mouth.

"What happened?"

"I-I-I'm not sure," he stammered. "I don't remember much. The guys, they grabbed me and said it was time for me to prove my loyalty and join the brotherhood. They pulled me out of my room and then knocked me out. When I woke up, I was tied to this chair."

"What is that?" Lance asked, pointing to a small black box on the closet floor.

"I-I don't know. It was dark in there, so I couldn't see anything," the student answered, rubbing his freshly freed wrists.

"Get out of the building as fast as you can," Lance ordered before turning his attention back to the closet as the student ran out, running into desks, chairs, and anything else that was between him and the door as he rushed out of the lab.

He moved the fallen chair the student had been sitting on to reach the box. He opened it to find what he had expected but feared: Fox's bomb. Attached to it, he found a timer reading two minutes and fifteen seconds.

"Help me out here, Taylor." He stood the chair back up and sat in front of the bomb.

"Pick it up. I need to be able to see all of it."

Lance did what he was told, spinning the bomb three hundred and sixty degrees horizontally and then vertically.

"This is where we really needed Jason," he said after fifteen seconds of Lance spinning the bomb in front of his suit camera.

"Taylor, I need you to concentrate. In one minute and forty-five seconds, this bomb, this building, myself, and anyone else near this place will blow up. Unless you tell me how to stop it."

"I don't know. That's the problem. There aren't any wires, any switches. It is just a small gray box with a timer. Whatever could disarm it is inside of that box, but if you open it, you risk it exploding anyway. You need to leave. Now."

"Not happening." Lance turned the box over and picked at where two pieces met, opening the box.

"It's two pieces. Just a shell covering the bomb itself. We have one minute left. Do you see anything now?"

"Lance, I'm not a weapons guy. I'm a tech guy. I don't know how to help you right now except to tell you to leave while you have a chance."

"This is tech, Taylor!" he shouted, a bead of sweat running down his temple. "It has to be connected to some wireless crap, right? Can't you disarm it remotely?"

"I've been trying to do that since you talked to Fox. There is no signal coming from the bomb. Everything connected to it is in your hands. You have to leave right now. Twenty-five seconds would be lucky to get you out the door."

Lance stood and placed the bomb on the chair, and took a step away, shaking.

"No. No! I can't leave. There's no way everyone is out of here. I have to try."

Lance closed his eyes and unsheathed his sword, illuminated by the electric current to the same bright white as his suit. He took a deep breath that quaked as he exhaled. *Now or never*, he thought, opening his eyes back up. He reached the sword up over the bomb and thrust it back down into the bomb with the electricity still flowing through the sword, closing his eyes and wincing as he felt the tip come into contact with the bomb.

"Lance, no!" Taylor exclaimed as he realized what Lance was doing.

But it was too late.

The sword had entered the bomb with no resistance, diving into it as if it were water.

Nothing happened. Lance opened his eyes to find the timer had stopped at five seconds. He slumped into the chair, relieved but still shaking. He leaned back into the chair and let out a deep exhale. *We did it.* He opened his mouth, excited to celebrate with Taylor, excited to revel in their success in defusing the bomb, excited that they were in the clear now, that they had saved the day, but he couldn't hear his own words. They were drowned out by the roar of an explosion and the groaning of the building as it shook and began to crumble. Lance toppled out of the chair with a ringing in his ears until everything around him went silent. Silent and dark.

chapter

TWENTY-FIVE

Lance opened his eyes. It was still as dark as it had been when they were closed. Blinking rapidly, he tried to get the dust out of his eyes floating up into his mask. He struggled to push himself up, but a huge weight bore down on top of him, making it difficult to move even an inch.

Lance struggled to remember how much time had passed since the explosion. He remembered falling from the chair, and a chorus of noises as the building around him fell. He remembered feeling a weight land on top of him and having the breath knocked out of him. *But how long has it been since then?* He asked himself, shaking his head. It could have been a matter of seconds or hours. Lance didn't think he had blacked out but wouldn't bet money on that.

He stretched his arms out in front of him, feeling for something, anything, to grab hold of to pull himself out of the rubble. He finally found a chunk of what must have been part of the concrete wall to grasp, and he pulled himself a few inches before his arms locked out. He pulled again at the chunk. And again. He pulled until his arms locked out, and then he'd pull again. He pulled until his body was halfway out from under the weight on top of him. Lance tried to use the piece of the wall to pull further but had pushed himself as far as this piece would allow. He patted around for another handhold but came up empty, as everything within reach was too light to serve his needs. He tried rolling onto his side but to no avail. The wall had his legs pinned. After resting a moment to catch his breath, Lance began trying to pry the weight off of him, turning the sword on its side to lift the wall off of him, if only an inch.

There wasn't enough room for the prying to do much good, but it allowed him to squirm out enough to find something else to hold the weight of the wall. He wiggled and pulled himself out an inch at a time, dropping his sword to use both hands to pull himself out from under the wall. Lance finally got back on his feet after several minutes of struggling. He patted himself, trying to find any injuries from the explosion. He winced as his hand touched his chest, a sharp pain stabbing from his ribs. His ankle still hurt, but it was no worse than earlier. He moved his hands to his head and found a crack from the center of the helmet on the back of his head, tracing diagonally down to his right ear, but it seemed the helmet was still intact. He wouldn't be able to check the rest of his suit until he made it out into the light. He could dimly see the rubble of the lab around him, but just through beams of light pouring in from the outside now that the building had crumbled in on itself.

"Taylor," he spoke loudly into his headset. "Taylor, can you hear me? Taylor, come in."

There was no response. Not even static. *Looks like I'm on my own.* He bent down on one knee and searched for his sword. He found the handle after a moment of looking, but the blade was still lodged under the weight that had been on top of him. He sat and grasped his sword in his hands as he placed his feet against the slab he had been under. He pushed at the wall with his legs and pulled on the sword simultaneously. After three tries, he could finally pull the sword out. Standing up, the sword illuminated the room.

Lance opened his mouth, but nothing came out. All he could see was rubble, like the ruins of some forgotten city. One wall remained standing, keeping a tiny area from being demolished, but the rest of the room had been destroyed. Had Lance been five feet further from the wall, he would have been crushed. He limped over to the door that was still standing in the lone wall and opened it.

A sliver of light came through the cracks of the fallen building and Lance let his sword go dark. He sheathed it and began trying to dig a way out. Initially, he tried to reach the light, but with each piece he removed, two more took its place, threatening to take him out as well in the process. Lance's new plan was to reach the stairwell right across the hall.

Slowly, he was able to create a space just large enough for himself to squeeze through by removing the smaller pieces between himself and the stairs. He continued on at this pace until fifteen minutes later; he found the door frame intact but with the door missing. The stairwell had debris in it but had withstood the explosion better than he could've imagined after seeing the remains of the lab and the hallway. He had to watch his step going up, but he didn't have to move any debris to get up the stairs. He opened the stairwell door on the ground floor and stepped outside into a blinding light.

The building had collapsed entirely. Four stories of concrete, tile, wood, and whatever else the building had been made of were strewn about his feet. Desks and chairs, both intact and broken into pieces, littered the ground. He looked to the other side of the collapsed building and saw flames still leaping from the ruins as the fire department continued to douse it. The building just beyond the flames was also crumbling. The explosion had been close enough to take a chunk out of it as well. People ran in and out of that building, carrying wounded students out. He watched as Ashley came into view. She was helping another student make it to the triage area that had been set up while he was in the lab before returning to help more students. He let out a sigh of relief at the sight of her and tried again to contact Taylor, hoping that being out from the rubble would free the signal, but there was still nothing from the headset.

Then Lance's heart stopped. He saw Sam run out of the building with a small, light-brown-haired girl in his arms, signaling for the medics to help him. He wasn't close enough to actually see for himself, but he knew that the girl was Gwen. His fears were confirmed as he saw Jason and Hailey hobble out of the building, holding on to one another and heading straight to where Sam was with the girl still in his arms.

Lance leaped from one large piece of debris to another to get out of the wreckage before Jason looked up and saw him. He shook him off. He motioned for the building and walked that way, separating from Hailey, who kept following Sam and Gwen. Lance froze. He understood what Jason was trying to tell him. Rushing to Gwen's side would give away his secret to anyone interested, Fox included. His identity would be out there for all to see. Whereas going straight from crawling out of the ruins of a collapsed building to trying to rescue students from a building still in the process of collapsing would undoubtedly be the heroic thing to do at the moment, something that would be expected of the White Knight.

But it's Gwen, he thought as he continued watching Sam direct an ambulance to where she was.

The choice was made for him as the medics loaded Gwen into the ambulance and closed the doors. Hailey crawled into the back with her, and Sam took off toward the still crumbling chemistry building, trying to find more students in the debris. Lance took off in a jog to catch Jason right as he walked into the building.

"Is she okay?" he asked in a low voice as more students rushed out of the building, doing a double take as they passed him but continuing on their way away from the rubble.

"I think so," Jason responded, reaching up to massage his neck as they walked up the stairs, alone now. "She fell out of her seat and hit her head when the explosion happened. It knocked her out, and she hadn't regained consciousness by the time we were able to make it out. They held us in the room for fifteen minutes to make sure there wasn't going to be some kind of attack on the students when they rushed out of the building. Sam and Hailey tried to wake her, but she was out pretty hard. Some day for Sam to choose to hang out in class with us."

"What about you? I saw you and Hailey limping. Are y'all okay?"

"Yeah, we're fine. After the explosion happened, people were kind of freaking out. A guy ran into Hailey, jamming her against the desk, and someone else tripped into my legs, taking me down and spraining my ankle. I'll be fine, though. What happened?"

"Fox told me there was a bomb in the lab, acting as if he were helping, so I had to leave him to go for the bomb. I was able to disarm it, but there must have been at least one other bomb in the building. Jason, I rescued a student who was tied up with the bomb I found. There had to have been another student with the other bomb. That student will be found dead, Jason, if there's anything even left of him. And it's my fault," Lance said, shivering in his armor. "We had the chance to stop this, all of this, from happening Friday night, but I stopped you instead."

"You're right, and I never properly thanked you for that. This isn't on your hands any more than it is on mine. The only one to blame for this is Fox. Fox is a killer, but that doesn't mean we can become killers ourselves. That's not our place in this. To be the executioners isn't what we signed up for. We do what is right. We can't become like him to stop him. All that would do is create more of him."

They continued through the building, Jason's words hanging in the silence. Lance knew he was right, but he couldn't shake the guilt. *I started this to protect Gwen and the rest of the campus, but now I'm looking for injured students as Gwen is being rushed to the hospital, and the campus is in flames. What if I'm creating more problems than I'm solving?* He asked himself as they entered the last room in the building.

It, too, was empty. They exited the building to return to the mess outside. Blaring sirens were all they could hear. The stench of smoke was all they could smell. And the destruction of their campus was all they could see.

chapter

TWENTY-SIX

A DAY FOR MOURNING

Our campus fell under attack yesterday. Seventy-four of our classmates and professors passed away as a result of the terrorist attack on our school yesterday that saw both the chemistry building and Mulder Hall fall. Hundreds more are injured. The entire campus is grieving. There is hurt and heartbreak in our home, but we are fortunate to have two men watching over us.

Matthew Fox, CEO of Fox Industries, was present on campus for the bombings yesterday and has pledged to aid the university in rebuilding what has fallen in any way he can. "Money isn't something I care much about. I know that's something you always hear people who have too much of it say, but for me, it's true. The final number in my bank account will not affect what I give to this university. I will give however much it needs. I believe in this school. I see the compassion and unity the students here have shown in the wake of this tragedy, and it strengthens me to know that this generation coming up is more than what the media presents it as."

Fox also had unsolicited praise for our other guardian, the White Knight. After praising the campus and city first responders, Fox added, "It takes a special kind of resolve to walk into a room with a bomb in it, knowing you might die, to try and save others that will never know who you are. I couldn't have done what he did. As those security tapes have shown, this man only fears death in so much as it affects those around him. That is a good man. There aren't many of those in the world today. Don't take it for granted. There's no way of knowing how long someone like that will be around. This man should be treated as a hero, not the criminal he's been painted as. There's no way to know how many lives were spared thanks to his courageous act. We are all indebted to his courage."

With our two heroes watching over this campus, we can feel protected again. That doesn't mean we will be safe; nothing can guarantee our safety, but it does mean evil will have its hands full in making its way to us. And that's all we can hope for.

Writing for the last time for the Franklin Gazette.

Hailey Hall

"How did you find the time to write this, Hall? You haven't left this room for more than ten minutes since she was admitted," Lance asked Hailey as the two sat with Gwen in her hospital room.

She had a concussion and fractured ribs, but the doctors said they would likely release her later tonight after the CT scans come back as long as everything checks out, just over twenty-four hours since being admitted.

Hailey and Sam had escaped unscathed while Jason's sprained ankle was causing him to walk with a limp, but it wasn't something worth taking attention away from the more severe injuries suffered by other students. Taylor had offered to tape his ankle to keep it secure, but Jason opted just to use a brace he would use during intramurals.

Lance also had two fractured ribs that Taylor diagnosed and treated once he had gotten back to the base. He was wearing a compression wrap under his shirt while it healed. He had also suffered a sprained ankle and a mild concussion, but there wasn't much Taylor could do for those. Taylor had offered the same taping for Lance's ankle, but Lance did without. He had been lucky to escape with such minor injuries after having a building fall on him. *Luckier than most of the other students who hadn't made it out before it fell.*

"She was asleep ninety percent of the time. It wasn't too difficult once I got Sam and Taylor to shut up."

Gwen smiled from where she was propped up in the bed as Hailey talked, happy to have her friends there with her in her pain. She was even happy to hear them bickering again. It had been too long since they had been together like this.

"Speaking of which, where did David and Goliath go?"

"My actual biblical name of Samson isn't good enough for you?" Sam asked as he and Taylor entered the room with armfuls of vending machine snacks, handing them out like Christmas presents.

"I think the comparisons work," Taylor said with a shrug as he sat at the foot of Gwen's bed, handing her a candy bar.

"The great king Taylor," Sam laughed. "'The White Knight has taken out his thousands, and Sir Taylor his tens of thousands.' That's what all of the women of Franklin sing, isn't it?"

"Something like that," Taylor said with a small grin, taking a drink from his water bottle.

The room fell silent as they each opened their snacks. They tried being optimistic, but with a morgue full of wounded students and a the hospital around them filled with even more, it felt wrong. There wasn't much to be optimistic about at the moment. They had done all they could, and who knows how many lives were saved by stopping the second bomb, but there was still the looming sense of loss hanging over everything. Fox had won. Any evidence linking him to creating the drugs or the bomb had gone to the ground with the chemistry building.

Why? Lance thought to himself. *Why would he use the campus in the first place? Why couldn't he just use his own labs? Why couldn't he just have had the lab wiped down?* It didn't add up for Lance. There was no reason for all this devastation. Jason walked into the room. He picked up the remote, turned the volume up, and crossed his arms. Everyone turned to the screen as Fox spoke to start the ten o'clock news.

"What happened to this university is a tragedy. But this university is strong, and Fox Industries stands strong with the Franklin family. The chemistry building was the last nameless building on the campus, but no more. The Matthew Fox Chemistry Hall and Research Center will break ground the moment the ruins from the bombing are cleared. I vow to make this new building one of the nation's foremost chemistry centers. We will rebuild, and we will be stronger for it."

Fox stepped from the mic as applause broke through the crowd. His face broke into a triumphant smirk as he waved to the crowd. A hero. That's what the public saw. A man coming to the rescue in this university's time of need. This was why he blew up the building. He needed to be seen as a hero, a champion of the people, so he could have the approval he needed to start his war to end all wars.

Lance felt bile attempting to come up into his mouth. He pressed it back as a man in a suit came up to the stage to whisper into Fox's ear. Fox nodded to the man and stepped back to the mic, motioning for the crowd to quiet as he did so.

"I've just been told that the university has accepted our proposal to provide vaccinations to the entirety of the student body. Our team, led by your esteemed professor, Dr. Jacobsen, has worked tirelessly to collect samples from the air surrounding ground zero. With the chemicals in the building and with the experiments being run there, we were worried about the possibility of illness, and our test results have shown that we were wise to do so. President Arnold has asked every student to get the vaccine sometime next week. Even if you were not in the area, we urge you to come by as a precaution. Thank you for your time." He stepped away from the microphone to more applause and hurriedly walked off with his entourage.

Jason muted the television.

"What a great gesture," Gwen mumbled from her bed.

She had lain back down, her medicine kicking back in.

"Yep. A real stand-up guy," Jason answered, arms crossed and leaning against the door frame.

"You don't seem too enthused with your future employer trying to rescue your current school. Most people would be pretty thrilled that a billionaire was coming to their aid," Hailey remarked, turning her chair to face him and raising an eyebrow.

"I just think it an odd coincidence that he happened to be on campus right before the bombing. Especially since the security tapes that leaked showed the White

Knight having to untie a student near the bomb instead of coming across the bomber like Fox had told him he would."

"So, what? You think Fox was the bomber?"

"I don't think it's too far out there to think that he could have been involved, no."

Sam stood, slapping his thighs as he did so, and made his way to the door. "Well, I think this conversation has taken a turn for the crazy. I have to move the last of my stuff to Duncan in the morning to my new place. I've got to get up early, so I'm going to turn in early tonight. I will see all y'all when you get to Duncan in a few weeks. Hailey," he said, giving Hailey, who had stood, a hug as she whispered, "Bye, Sammy."

"Gentlemen." He shook each of their hands. He looked back into the room as he left. "Take care of her," he said, motioning to Gwen, who had fallen back asleep, and with that, he was gone.

"We should be heading out as well," Lance said, rising. "Let us know when you get her home, Hall. And don't hesitate to call if either of you need anything."

"Of course."

Taylor patted her shoulder, and Jason gave her a quick kiss as they left the room. It was almost dead week, with a little over a week until finals started. However, as they had learned last semester, that didn't signify a drop in violence. The White Knight would not get the night off.

Lance inevitably felt his stomach drop as he walked down the hall lined with beds. The hospital didn't have enough rooms for everyone being treated after the explosion. Patients with severe injuries had been taken to Duncan, but even with that number gone, the hospital was still overrun. The knowledge that he had done all he could wasn't enough to keep his overwhelming guilt at bay.

"What do you think about this vaccine he's offering, Taylor?" Lance asked, trying to get his mind on something more helpful than wallowing in the pain surrounding him.

"I think it's legit," Taylor answered with a shrug. "Dad is pretty close to the university's chief medical officer. For this to be offered to the whole student body, he has to have signed off on it, so I trust it. I'll reach out to him to make sure this is something he's pushing and let you know what he says. I'll for sure be getting mine if he's recommending it."

Lance nodded. He didn't know nearly enough about this sort of thing. If Taylor vouched for it, he'd get the vaccine, no matter how sick it made him take Matthew Fox's charity after what he had done.

chapter

TWENTY-SEVEN

There had been no action that night, nor would there be any incidents for the next two and a half weeks to come. The bombing, along with finals week wrapping up, seemed to deter most of the rowdiness they had grown accustomed to facing. So, they finished their senior year in a much more mundane manner than they had spent the rest of the semester to the point that it was almost normal.

Almost, but not quite, Lance thought to himself. There were still too many reminders of his work as the White Knight over the last few weeks of classes for him to consider it normal. They still spent almost every night in the storage unit, even if they made more time for Gwen and Hailey than they had previously. There were still the lingering injuries they all held to varying degrees as Gwen continued to recover from her injuries and Lance's ribs were slow to heal, though Lance and Jason's ankle had both healed with the opportunity to rest.

The biggest reminder, though, was the remains of the chemistry building they had to walk by every day. The campus population was still subdued as the semester closed, but in the last week or so, some energy returned to the campus as talking and laughter could be heard from pockets of campus even if it wasn't as loud as had been the previous month. But that wasn't the case surrounding the chemistry building, where rubble remained as a rotating cast of construction crews cleared the area. Even with Fox bankrolling the work, there was only so much the crews could do in such a short time.

But, for the most part, they spent their final days as college students as just college students and nothing more. They studied for tests and took finals. They had a couple of movie and game nights and worked on packing up their belongings before leaving Franklin behind. Now, graduation was the only thing left for them to cross off their college checklist before leaving.

Lance walked back to the apartment to get his truck after getting breakfast at the cafeteria on Friday morning with Jason and Taylor, a last meal where they had so often eaten together over the previous four years . . . He was going to pick Gwen and Hailey up to get their vaccinations. Fox might be an evil man, but Lance wasn't willing to risk his friends suffering from some unknown illness for his vendetta against Fox. *He will get what is coming to him*, Lance told himself. It was the last day of finals week, and Taylor and Jason still had one last final to take, so they had stayed on campus to do some last-minute cramming before their tests. They had gotten their vaccination on Monday when the clinic had first made it available. Gwen's doctors ordered her to wait as long as possible to allow her other medication to wear off so that there weren't any setbacks, so Lance and Hailey had waited to get theirs so they could go with her.

They arrived at the vaccination tables at the campus clinic and waited in line for an hour and a half. With every student having to be vaccinated, the small clinic was at full capacity, and the line stretched out the door and halfway around the block, longer than the lines for the campus's sporting events. By the time they were finally finished at the clinic, the three were starving, so they headed toward the student union and found it deserted. With all but a handful of finals finished, most students had rushed off for the summer. They each ordered a burger basket and found an empty table to sit down at with their lunch.

"Have you two finished packing yet?" Lance asked before taking a bite from his burger.

"We finished yesterday. Hailey's parents are driving into Duncan tomorrow, and they're renting a moving truck to help us get everything to our new place in the city. My parents will come over tomorrow too and bring my dad's truck to take some of the smaller stuff with them."

"My parents think we can make it in one trip, but I am just really hoping it will only take two," Hailey laughed.

"Are you guys packed yet?"

"Yeah, Jason and I moved all of our stuff into Taylor's dad's house in Duncan. We think we have a place to stay there but won't find out for certain for another week or so. Taylor's dad is supposed to be in Europe through the end of the month, so we're just staying at the house until we can move into the new place. We mainly just have the essentials for the weekend here now. Can you believe we graduate tomorrow? And by next week, we'll be living in a new city?"

"Have you found a job yet?" Hailey asked.

"Not yet." Lance shook his head and finished chewing the bite he had taken before he continued. "I'm still waiting to see if I'm going to get into the grad program in Duncan. They will let the people on the waitlist know next week sometime. Still, it's rough being the only one without a plan. When do you start again?"

"A week from Monday," Hailey answered. Gwen had almost finished her burger and had started eating Lance's fries.

"I don't know anyone else starting this month," Lance laughed.

"It's not like you know that many people, Locke," Hailey pointed out.

"Fair point, Hall. And I'm glad to see you have your appetite back," he said to Gwen, who had just finished his fries.

"Maybe if you weren't talking so much, you could have had some, too. I would've shared."

"How generous of you." Lance rolled his eyes and fought off a smile. "Come on," he said, rising to his feet. "It's already almost four. We need to go find Taylor and Jason before commencement this evening."

The girls stood, and the three of them all headed back to the guys' apartment together in Lance's truck. Taylor was already there, getting dressed in his suit. Taylor had taken his four-point GPA throughout his college career and was to give a short speech along with the other three Magna Cum Laude seniors. Jason hadn't returned from his last test yet, so it was just Taylor in the apartment when they arrived. Lance grabbed Hailey and himself a bottle of water before they collapsed on the couch, both putting their feet up on the coffee table in front of them. Gwen helped Taylor with his tie and fussed with his hair as he squirmed under her attention. She stepped back and smiled once she was satisfied.

"How do I look?" he sheepishly asked.

"Stunning," Hailey answered.

"Absolutely breathtaking," Lance added right as Jason walked through the door.

"Taylor wants to know how he looks," Hailey quipped as he sat his bag down.

Jason looked him up and down.

"Stunning."

"Taken," Lance answered as Hailey lifted her arm and pointed down at herself.

"Hmmm. Let's go with cute as a button then," Jason said, pinching Taylor's cheeks as he walked by, causing Taylor to squirm again as he swatted Jason's arm away.

"Don't listen to them," Gwen told him, straightening his tie again. "Auntie would be proud."

Taylor smiled and hugged Gwen. He wiped a tear from his eye and checked his watch.

"We should probably be leaving. Are you all ready?"

"Let's roll," Jason said, helping Hailey to her feet with one hand and pushing Lance back onto the couch with the other as the five all headed to the arena.

Saturday, they saw each other only briefly as they each had their own graduation ceremony to attend. Gwen's parents came and watched her ceremony, and Taylor's since his dad was still in Europe after telling Taylor he would be at his medical school graduation, which was the only one that mattered. Hailey's and Jason's parents attended both ceremonies and spent the day together. Lance's mom came to watch his ceremony but told him his dad had to take an extra shift and could not attend, though she promised him he had wanted to.

The next day, the guys helped Hailey and Gwen pack up the moving truck and clean their house before the landlord arrived to pick up the key. After the girls drove off, they packed the last of their belongings and loaded them into Lance's truck. They stopped at the storage unit before leaving for Duncan.

The room felt eerie now that their time on campus had ended. They hadn't moved anything out of the base yet, but it was as if the room knew that a chapter had ended.

"What do we do now?" Jason asked, running his hand across his red suit before following Lance back to the door. "We made this campus better, but we're leaving it now. What happens to all of this?"

Lance locked the door to the storage unit behind them and answered as they climbed into his truck. "Someone once told me that you have to fight for a better future. That the future can always be made better. So, where do we go from here? We go to Duncan. And we find a way to stop Matthew Fox. That's what we do."

Acknowledgements

I can't believe this book exists. At it's release in April 2024, it has been in my mind in some form for almost exactly a decade.

In 2014, as a sophomore at the University of Oklahoma, I went to a renaissance fair to get extra credit for my Latin class. My one goal for the trip was to buy a sword. The following weekend I got sick watched the first season-and-a-half of Arrow over a 36 hour span and my main takeaway was that it would be so much cooler if a hero used a sword like the one I had just bought instead of a bow and arrow. That turned into a conversation with the people on my dorm floor about what it would look like to create a "superhero" major. What would the classes be or a capstone look like if the goal was to become a superhero after graduation.

Those conversations led to a short story called The Night Watchman which was not at all good and I have ensured there is no paper trail proving its existence. But that short story became the inspiration for the first scene in The White Knight where Lance fights the man in the courtyard. I wrote the first draft in 2015 and it was only thirty-five thousand words and was almost as bad as the short story. A few more rewrites got it to forty-five thousand mediocre words.

Then in 2020, I decided to revisit the world. I added twenty thousand words and did major edits on what I already had to get this book that I can be proud of releasing. That was the first time I started to really look into what it would take to publish it. And now its here. I've always loved the stories superheroes tell but I've always preferred novels to comics. With The White Knight, I have gotten to write the book I always wanted to read.

The existence of this book ten years after its inception wouldn't be possible without the help and support of so many people in my life.

My wife, Taylor, has been my number one supporter and has pushed me to not let fear of failure keep me from making this book a reality. This book would likely still exist only in my head without her support.

I need to thank my mom and dad for their constant support as well. From the time I learned how to read they have always encouraged my love for it, even if there were still the occasional "he lives!" comments when I would emerge from binge reading. They have always made me believe I could accomplish anything I could dream and made me believe I was capable of doing something like this for my entire life.

I have had so many friends that have supported and encouraged me and I know I couldn't hope to list them all here. Special thanks to my friends that read my stories before they were professionally edited and gave me indispensable feedback: Ashlyn, Bronson, Emily, Nick, Taylor. More thanks to friends who either answered writing questions or social media questions as I tried to write and market this book: Haley, Maddie, Steven. Finally, while I won't list them all, I never would have come up with these stories if it wasn't for my time living in campus housing during undergrad so a special thanks to Muldrow 6, Muldrow 9, and the Couch RA staff that I got to live with and talk with about superheroes seemingly every day.

Lastly, I want to thank the people who made my book professionally polished and presentable. My editors, Samantha Pico and Haley Larkin, made this infinitely more readable. MIBL Art made me a cover I love and did all my formatting.

About the Author

K.B. Kirtley is an author from Oklahoma writing the stories he always wanted to read. K.B. holds a lifelong love of superheroes and reading but has always struggled to fall into comics the same way he has with books. His debut series combines the kind of stories he loves in the format he most connects with in a collection of books and short story series introducing a new universe of superheroes.

To keep up to date on all news on upcoming books, find links to all social accounts, and for free access to The Street Rat and all future short story series, go to KirtleyBooks.com.

Turn the page for the first
two episodes of:

The
Street Rat

The Street Rat is free to read
at kirtleybooks.com

The Street Rat 101

"Ba-dada-da."

Eddie Danson skirted across the uppermost ledge of the soot-covered brownstone apartment building, seven stories above the cramped streets of Sanders.

"What's a superhero without a theme song?" he pondered out loud to himself and the pigeons that littered the rooftop to his right, edging forward along the crumbling ledge of the old building.

"Well, maybe not a superhero, per se. Just a normal hero. That will have to suffice for now, since I haven't been lucky enough to come across any radiation," he lamented. Shaking his head at his poor luck, he searched for a consoling look from the expressionless pigeons sitting on top of the humming A/C unit. "Lawless vigilante also has a nice ring to it. That's how the Sanders Police Department refers to me, so it has some authority behind it as well. And they've already gone to the trouble of making fan art of me, hanging posters around town. Even though they have no idea what I look like."

He squatted as he reached the corner of the building, pulling out one of the wanted posters he had kept carefully folded in his chest pocket. "Nose is too small. Eyes too far apart. Hair is completely off. Stan culture is wild." He gestured as he talked to the pigeon sitting next to him on the ledge.

A siren blared a block away, joining the symphony of sirens providing Sanders its soundtrack, causing the pigeon to fly off to another roof.

"Best not to get too hung up on the title anyway." Putting the paper back in his pocket, he sighed. "A rose by any other name can still draw blood, or something like that."

"Get back!"

The woman's scream, more of a threat than a cry for help, came up from the alley beneath him.

After leaping ten feet from his building to the one across the alley, he grabbed a rusty fire escape. With graffiti racing by in front of him, he dropped from the outside railing of one landing to the next, then landed less than fifteen seconds after the scream.

He surveyed the scene as he crept up to the party from behind. The only light in the alley came from the streetlight at the entrance, leaving most of the street covered in shadows.

Two men with knives hovered over a young woman and two children. Both men were a few inches taller than he was, but as a five-foot-six sixteen-year-old, he had gotten used to that being the case.

Maybe I'll hit that mythical growth spurt one day.

The woman was shorter than him, with long black hair falling to one side of her brown face. The boys had short black hair and the same complexion as the woman. The only noticeable difference between the two in the dim lighting was the one in the back was shorter than the one directly behind the woman.

She clutched her small bag in her right hand, waving it back and forth in front of the men as a weapon, though the jingling change lessened its intimidation. The jingle, however, mixed with the ongoing sirens and the hum of the A/C units sticking out of every other window, was enough to keep the men from detecting Eddie's footsteps as he closed in on them from behind.

He kicked the man to his right in the back of the knee, sending him toppling to the ground with a shout, before lunging for the other mugger. With a grunt and a thud, the two landed on the pavement as he rolled over the mugger.

"Brought a knife to a fist fight, I see," he observed, pinning the mugger's knife hand to the ground with his foot while the man's eyes widened in fear and fury. "That doesn't hardly seem fair."

Turning to the young woman and two boys, he sighed.

"That's the issue with criminals today. They no longer understand honor. Makes me yearn for the days of yore with men who at least had a code when they stole from you. Alas…" He shrugged before delivering a succession of punches to the mugger's face, leaving him limp.

He looked up to see the second mugger hobbling out of the alley on his one good leg. Leaping to his feet, he cut off the injured man, delivering another round of punches but holding the wit this time.

My deadliest weapon.

He dragged the body back to where the man's comrade had fallen and dropped him as he checked on the young woman and children he had so valiantly fought to protect.

"Are you all right, little lady?" he asked in his best southern accent, tipping his imaginary hat, drawing from the old Westerns he had watched as a kid.

Always nice to be chivalrous after saving a damsel in distress. Rule number one.

"Tonto!" the woman cried out, hitting the man in the arm with her purse as the little boys laughed. "You could've gotten us all hurt! Or we could've been thrown in prison, Eddie!"

"Relax, Maria," Eddie answered with a smile. "I promised your mother I'd look out for you and the boys while she was gone, and the Danson men are men of their word." Fisting his right hand, he pounded his chest once for emphasis before approaching the two unconscious men. "Now, it's time for the cruel mistress irony to join us."

"Why do you talk like that? It doesn't even make sense…" Maria sighed as she walked over to join Eddie by the fallen muggers.

"It's poetic," Eddie responded, bending to one knee as he emptied the first mugger's pockets. "When they write my biography, they'll need good quotes to use from my time at every stage in life. I can see the title of the second or third chapter now."

He closed his eyes, spreading his hands out in front of him. "Poetry in Poverty. I'm going to be such an inspiration to the homeless teen demographic publishers are dying to cater to."

"Not if you die before you can do anything worthy of a biography."

Eddie stood, looked at her for a moment, and shrugged. "They would still make great quotes in my obituary. Here." He dropped a knife and thirty-seven dollars into Maria's bag, holding onto a pocket watch for himself. "Who knew pocket watches were still such a fundamental accessory to a life of crime? I can't imagine the success I'd be enjoying if I'd only had a pocket watch sooner."

"Are you going to search the other mugger, too, or are we going to have to do this again tomorrow night?"

"Oh, ye of little mercy. What would Rosa say if she saw how cruel her daughter had become?"

"Not nearly as much as she would say when she found out you were running around, stopping crime and then stealing from the thieves themselves. And using her children you 'swore to protect' as bait."

Eddie handed her the knife and twenty-one dollars he pulled from the second man.

"We're coming away from this with only fifty-eight dollars, a pocket watch, and two knives. That's not enough value to really be considered stealing, is it?"

"We could leave with nothing but some loose change and a button, and it would still be stealing. That's how stealing works."

"And besides," Eddie continued, "I take down a lot more crime in this city than I get money. I guarantee you I stop more crime than the average SPD officer, but they come away with a much bigger paycheck than fifty-eight lousy bucks for a night's work. But I guess I have the coolest job ever as a superhero, and they're just ordinary, boring cops, so it all evens out in the end."

"You're not a superhero. You don't have any powers."

"Details." He waved dismissively, taking a length of rope from one of the young boys. Eddie tied up each of the men and dragged them to the sidewalk.

"Now—" he crouched to eye level before the boys, "—who's ready for dinner?" He raised his eyebrows.

The boys nodded along furiously to what Eddie was saying. "Maria?" All three looked up to where their sister was still standing with her hands on her hips, each making puppy-dog eyes to varying levels of success.

"Yeah, okay. Let's go get some dinner."

Eddie gave the older boy a high-five and ruffled the younger's hair as he stood and followed them out of the alley and into the light alongside Maria.

"I need to come up with a name and a costume. They don't give biography deals to anonymous heroes without a costume. It would be unbecoming."

"You could be the Street Rat instead of just being a street rat," Maria answered with an eye roll. "You could wear whiskers and a tail. Surely that would get you a biography."

"I'm not so sure about the costume idea, seems a bit too 1960s silliness, and I expect more from my director of public relations, but 'The Street Rat' would be a fantastic name. That's a great start, Maria. Now, all I need is a costume, one that could preferably incorporate this new pocket watch." He dropped the watch into his jacket pocket. With a flourish. "Professionalism is of the utmost importance in my line of work."

Eddie opened the diner door, welcoming the cool air and the smell of greasy food. The bell above the door rang as it closed behind him while he followed all he'd ever really had for a family in for a late dinner at Sal's.

The Street Rat 102

"Please, sir." The young boy's voice quivered as he spoke. "I only have three dollars. I am supposed to bring back soup cans so that me and my mama can eat dinner this week."

"Do I's look like I's gonna care about some sad story like that, kid? Now, hands it over before I's have to take its from you," the burly man growled, brandishing his knife again in the alley he had pulled the kid into.

It wasn't much darker in the alley than the street. Sanders had an acrid cloud of smog drifting permanently over the city from the thousand factories in the area. Even the most environmentally conscious politicians had given up fighting years ago at the risk of being run out of town.

"Absolutely atrocious."

Turning to find Eddie leaning against a wall with a piece of straw coming out of his mouth, the burly man left the kid where he was standing, but the child stood still.

Sirens blared in the distance, and boats honked in the bay to the east.

Not quite a desert whistle, but it'll do to score the showdown, I guess.

"What's thats you say?"

"Positively putrid," Eddie answered, pushing himself off the graffitied wall and walking over to join the man and the kid. "Do you have any idea how us talking like that causes others to view us? All those people out in the cushy suburbs think they're better than you and I. It's all a sham, though, really, don't you think, Buzz?"

"The name's Frank."

"My apologies, Francis. But you miss my point. They think they're better than us because they have these nice homes, these fancy jobs, these prestigious degrees. And so, they think we're dirt. But we aren't dirt, are we, Francis?"

"Nos. I guess not."

"That's absolutely right. And I'm not even talking about how we talk but rather how we speak to each other. We are just as much human as they are, and that means we have just the same value as them. But—" Eddie put his arm around Francis and turned him back to the small child, "—if we behave in the way they see us, we become just what they say we are. Not because of how they view us in relation to them, but how we become forced to view ourselves in relation to one another." Eddie paused to gesture from Francis to himself.

Do I talk with my hands too much? Eddie asked himself. I mean, I feel like it is helping me get my points across better, and I swear Francis looks to be softening up a bit to where I'll probably just end up in an ICU instead of a casket after my monologue, but still. Is it too gimmicky? I'm going to have to do market tests on this for when I hit it big. Get some focus group feedback. He probably gets the gesture thing now. I should talk again.

"Consider this child." Eddie guided Francis's vision from himself to the child with a wave of his hand. "How do you think this child views you, Francis? Do you think he views you as you are? As a human with worth and value? As someone who is a great and loyal friend for those lucky enough to know him? Or do you think he views you as a bad guy? A ruffian, if you will, who is not only a threat to his current safety with your knife but also a threat to his long-term security by taking away his dinner money? And if it's the second one, can you blame him?"

"I's didn't mean the little guy no harm. I's wasn't really gonna knife him," Francis explained, with what looked like a tear in his eye. "Youse know hows it is outs here, though. Just tryna takes cares of my own kids."

"And there's nothing wrong with that, Francis." Eddie rested his arm about four inches below Francis's hulking shoulder on the back of his leather vest. "We have to provide for those we care about, don't we? But there's other ways to do that. You know Jerry's? Down on the corner of Fifth and Walters? I know they're looking for someone who can help them keep trouble from breaking out down there. You'd be perfect for that. I'm sure Jerry would hire you on the spot."

"Eh, I's don't knows about that. Me and Jerry's got a history. I doubt he'd take me in."

"Now, listen to me, Frank. Can I call you Frank? You're not the same man you were then. You've changed. I know Jerry. He's a forgiving man. He loves giving out second chances. All you have to do is go to him and ask him for one."

"I's guess it's worth a shot. Better than taking foods from the kids outs here, huh?" Frank laughed as he patted the child on the shoulder. "I's don't really reckon I want to gives those guys outside the city the satisfaction of knowing theys better than me anyhow."

"Ah, that's the best part, Frank." Eddie smiled up at him. Time to bring it home. "They were never better than us. They steal from one another all the time. And they sacrifice each other's well-being for the smallest of personal comforts. They just obscure it with laws and yelling about rights. They were never actually better than us, but they feel better by thinking that. If they were to actually take the time to realize we are the same as them, then they would have to interact with us differently. It's much more comfortable for them to continue living as though the opportunities they get that we don't mean they are somehow more worthy of that.

"But, Frank, look what happened today. You put another person's needs to be safe and secure over your own. And, today, you are going to talk to Jerry and make things right so you can provide for your family. There is no one inside the city or outside the city that can look at you and say they have more worth or that they are better than you. I'd call that a good day."

Frank wiped a tear from his eye and patted Eddie on the back. "Youse alright, kid. What'd you say your name was again?"

"They call me the Street Rat."

"Sounds like one of thems comic book names. Youse one a thems superheroes?"

"I'm working on it." Eddie laughed. "If anyone asks, you can tell them I am. But for right now, I'm just trying to make our community better."

"Sounds likes a superhero to me, kid. I's best get goin' now. Jerry might could use some helps tonight, it being a Friday and all. I'll see ya around, kid."

"Good luck, Frank. It was nice talking to you."

Eddie put his arm on the child's shoulder and returned Frank's wave as he walked towards Jerry's.

"I'm going to miss that guy. I hope I see him around again. Now—" Eddie turned to look at the child as his face hardened "—give me your money."

The child stared up at him for a beat before they laughed.

"Come on, Tomas, Maria and Alex are probably getting worried that I got us both killed. Maria will probably be mad we didn't get any more money, but I think the two of us walking away without getting pummeled counts as a win, considering how that started. You could have a future as a movie star after that performance I just saw, and I have an eye for talent."

Eddie ruffled Tomas's black shaggy hair as they walked toward the diner to meet Maria and Alex.

"You really do have to give me that money back, though. Your sister would be furious if we don't get that back into the bag."

"Okay," Tomas said, coming to a stop and looking up at Eddie, "but one day this week, you have to take me to the Fry Farm. And I get to play on the playground! And I get to have a soda that I can refill!"

Eddie stopped and squatted in front of Tomas. He squinted hard at Tomas, stood back up, and laughed. "You drive a hard bargain, Tomas Delgado, but you've got yourself a deal. You know, Alex is going to have to go, too, though, right?"

"I'll allow it."

"I'm sure you will," Eddie laughed as he opened the door to the diner to follow Tomas in on the sticky floors, spotting Maria and Alex waiting for them in their booth.